CLAIMED BY THE SHEIKH

MOLLIE MATHEWS

CLAIMED BY THE SHEIKH

THE SHEIKHS UNTAMED BRIDES

MOLLIE MATHEWS

To my beloved partner, Lorenzo
and my daughter Hannah.

And for Cheryl and all the courageous men and women who
work in hostile environments to protect us all.

May you always be blessed with love,
freedom, and peace.

NOTE FROM THE AUTHOR

Dear Friends,

I hope you enjoy *Claimed by the Sheikh*. It touches on a number of subjects I love and care about with the twists and turns in the plot. I always love celebrating the strength of the human spirit, and what people do when faced with seemingly insurmountable challenges in their lives, and how unexpected events can turn disaster or tragedy into something good.

I love the fact that Melanie follows an unusual path as a pioneering architect. I love how hard she works at it. I always enjoy exploring how each of us uses and expresses our particular talents. And I felt a bond with her because I too studied architecture—but I didn't have the courage and determination that Melanie had to finish.

Watching Melanie struggle with discrimination, knock-backs, and success, and the price you pay for them, was familiar to me too. Each person lives success differently and her adventures along the way help her become the person she is destined to be. Whatever your path in life, you have a gift. Something nobody else can do as beautifully and skillfully as you.

How you express it, how you live it, and how you share it with others is unique to you. You have your own special way of dealing with life and the talents you've been given, whether you hide those gifts or share them openly.

I hope you enjoy reading about this talented young architect, and following her story as it unfolds. Victory and success come in many forms and guises, her path is an exciting, fascinating, and rewarding one, and I'm sure yours will be too!

With all my love,
Mollie

THE SECRET SHE KEPT FROM THE SHEIKH...

The secret she kept from the Sheikh...

A grief-stricken Sheikh Tariq na Hassir, the formidable ruler of the Kingdom of Avana, arrives in Paris to claim his brother's child after a car crash killed his parents--unaware that the child isn't their biological son. Salim is Tariq's son, with his former lover, a renowned architect.

Three years ago, after being banished by Tariq from his desert kingdom, Melanie Jones secretly gave her baby to Tariq's childless brother and his wife, in a swap the world was never supposed to know about.

The tragedy pulls her back to the world that rejected her and the man who abandoned her--the only man capable of turning her carefully controlled world upside down.

Tariq will do whatever it takes to protect his legacy, including claiming Melanie as his bride and his son as heir before scandals ensue.

But Melanie has other plans for her future—a westernized life where she's free to operate her own business and control her own life.

If you love true romance and beautiful love stories, set against a sensuous backdrop of the desert, art, and architecture you'll love *Claimed by The Sheikh.*

PRAISE FOR CLAIMED BY THE SHEIKH

"Wow, just wow, I can't articulate enough how compellingly page-turning this remarkable story was. If I could give it more than 5 stars this would be it! This author has the gift and the power to make you experience her remarkable craft on a whole other level. I was drawn into the story when she shared a few chapters with me quite a while ago now & I'm beyond thrilled that she managed to finish it. I'm not one to tell the story, the blurb & other reviewers will cover that but I will concede that this magical, mystical, hauntingly beautiful story will stay with me for the longest time. Highly recommended."

~ Terry Babb

"Claimed by the Sheikh was a fast-paced read that held my interest from the first page to the last. The story had a depth to the characters and strong imagery due to the author's attention to details. Watching two worlds collide, as well as two strong characters fight for what they each believe is right, just added another layer to the story.

I enjoy books that are set in the desert with desert royalty or sheikhs. Claimed by the Sheikh was a strong story with a depth to the characters of both Tariq and Melanie who we get to know a little at a time as well as their history from three years before. They seem to have unresolved issues and feelings for each other but given their differences will it be any different this time around? There was very strong imagery due to the vivid descriptions of the scenery, the palace and Melanie's drawings, which made me feel that I was there. Tariq's rescue of endangered animals and his philanthropy was a nice addition to the story. I liked how the child, Salim, was brought into the story as well as his importance to the storyline. Ms. Mathews is fast becoming a favorite author."

~ JoAnne

"This book grabbed me from the first page. Both lead characters were portrayed fully as real people not just by how they looked as in many books. There being a child involved added to my enjoyment!"

~ Melba

"The tone for this book is set in the opening chapters as the young Sheikh is faced with ongoing difficulties in the kingdom created by his atrocious father. He is fighting an ongoing battle to prevent himself from being sucked into the past and to rather create a new and prosperous future for his people. Tariq's previous rejection of Melanie and the results have soured her against romantic love and made her determined to carve a career for herself. "

~ Margaret

"I really like the premise of the book, I always like the royal romance with impediments to happiness and this book has it in spades. I like the strong figure of the Sheikh and the strong heroine who has built a professional career. Immediately I can see lots of problems that seem insurmountable at first: their past stormy relationship, the baby secret, her desire to have her own career, his desire for an heir, his demand to raise the child, his vow to swear off women. I also like that, right of the bat, we learn about his plan to build a reserve for animals and to right the many wrongs from his father's legacy. These are all good foundations for a fiery, passionate and conflicting relationship."

~ Elaine

"Fantastic premise that has a substantial conflict behind it. I like Melanie a lot. A strong female heroine is what I want to read. I think that is particularly important with such a powerful man, and here in this instance, someone who can wield such power. I love love love the beginning. This is one tough guy but the book opens with him protecting a baby giraffe. Fantastic opening."

~Leanne

"Tariq's emotional conflict is that he is in love with Melanie and won't admit it to himself. As a reader, it keeps me on pins and needles to see if Tariq realizes it himself."

~ Tonni

“It hooked me, it was impactful and well written. Sexual tension is always a plus for me and I loved the strong characters.”

~ Terry

“Claimed by the Sheikh has an intriguing plot: keeping the Sheikh's illegitimate child a secret through all the complications that arise. The main characters, Melanie as the independent architect and Tariq as the wealthy, powerful Sheikh of a fictitious Arab country are well fleshed out and believable. You have empathy for their situation and the tension about whether the secrets will be revealed carries you through the book. This is the stuff of fairy tales. The book does go a long way towards helping the reader understand Tariq's Islamic beliefs and his commitment to helping his people and the endangered animals he wants to rescue. There is a nice subplot about Melanie's struggle to become recognized as a creative architect in a field dominated by men. Tariq's wealth comes in handy there. A good heartfelt romance.”

~Elaine

An excellent story! The book pulled me in and I was completely engrossed from the first page until the last. This is the first book I've read by this author, and it will not be my last! I like how Tariq and Melanie, are shown on a real level and are both strong characters. The story is so well written, the plot flowed smoothly from page to page and the characters are captivating, have depth, and are well developed. A fantastic read and one I definitely recommend.

~ Lynn

PROLOGUE

The traffic on the motorway started to speed up as they got closer to Charlotte's husband's new office in the French headquarters of the Fédération Internationale de Football Association in southern France.

Salim was still asleep in the backseat when Charlie looked at her watch and realized it was nearly 1:00 am and they were going to be late to pick up Zayed. If he was exhausted, as he often was at the end of a long day, she knew he wouldn't wait.

He had been working so hard rebuilding his life to provide for her and Salim. Tonight had been a special celebration. She was proud that he had won the election to be the new FIFA president. His campaign focused on change, football ideals and uniting warring countries through their common passion for sport. She didn't want to be late.

Charlie grabbed her iPhone from the dashboard and placed it in her lap, to send him a text, when Salim suddenly woke.

"Don't drive and text, Mommy!" he said, disapprovingly. "You'll cause an accident."

"I just want to tell Daddy that we're running a few minutes late, but we're almost there. Otherwise, he'll grab a ride with one of his staff and leave before we arrive." Charlie looked down and started texting quickly, holding the steering wheel firm with one hand.

Ten minutes later Salim saw his father first as they approached the building where he worked. "Daddy!" Salim cried as Charlie pulled to the curb. She got out of the car and opened the passenger door. Salim had already unbuckled his seatbelt and climbed out of his booster seat. He ran to his father.

Zayed scooped him into his powerful arms and drew Charlie to his side. His sheer strength and physicality always made her swoon and she leaned into his chest.

"*Marhabaan, habibti*. Hello, my love. How's my favourite team?" he said, placing a kiss on Charlie's lips before turning to Salim and kissing his chubby cheeks.

"You must be tired," Charlie said.

Zayed heaved a deep breath, sucking the early morning air into his lungs. "Exhausted!"

"I'll drive," Charlie said. "Why don't you sit in the back and take a nap? I don't want you to be too tired to give me some special attention when we get home," she laughed, planting a sloppy kiss on his sexy lips.

She was thinking about Melanie and how grateful she was to her sister as she embraced Salim and Zayed. She wanted to take a selfie of them and send her a text but they agreed not to stay in contact. Those were the rules. Besides they had their own busy lives in separate worlds. She wasn't obliged to call, but she wanted to. But she didn't want to upset her or retraumatize her sister either. It wouldn't be fair to her. Not when Charlie was so happy, and Melanie was all alone.

Without Salim.

Charlie swallowed back the little trace of guilt that she never managed to kick and smiled as she watched Zayed clamber into the car, curling his long-powerful frame like a contortionist into the backseat. He waited for Salim to climb in and rested his head against the booster seat and fell asleep.

She was so happy. She didn't need to be a princess. She didn't need Zayed's royal title. All she needed was her two favourite men, she thought as she pressed the keyless start and pulled out from the curb.

Charlie wanted to get home quickly. Both her boys needed to be in their beds. She hadn't wanted to leave Salim with a babysitter and was feeling a little guilty for lifting him from his warm bed to pick up his dad, but she knew how much Zayed had missed them both. He had been working so hard and tonight had been a well-earned celebration. Thankfully their home was only a fast 40 minute trip on the A7 autoroute du Soleil.

They hadn't traveled far when Salim's eyes suddenly fluttered open. "You're not wearing your seatbelt!" he censured.

Charlie glanced at him in the rear-view mirror and noticed that Salim and Zayed weren't buckled in either. She'd heard the chime but had been distracted, worrying about Melanie, and how she must be suffering. Charlie been rushed and stressed all day.

"Neither are you," Charlie said, turning around.

"I forgot, mommy," Salim said, he rubbed his sleepy eyes and started to put his seatbelt on, but it was caught in the door and he couldn't. He tugged and pulled on it. "It's stuck, mommy."

Charlie's heart raced as she turned to keep her eyes on the road. She was sitting right on the legal speed limit of 80 mph. It always felt so fast. Behind and in front of her was a line of other cars and there was no room to pull over. She couldn't stop now, without causing an accident.

"We'll be home in a minute, darling," she said, glancing at Salim again in the rearview mirror. The words had barely left her mouth when his eyes flew wide open in horror. He saw a huge tourist bus careering toward them from the left.

PROLOGUE (CONT.)

Salim screamed. Charlie turned too late. The bus hit them with monstrous force.

Zayed woke and hurled his body across his son instinctively.

There was the sound of crushing metal and splintering glass as Charlie's cellphone flew from her hand. Salim watched in horror as his mother shot through the windshield like a torpedo. She careered through the air and disappeared under the cars in front. Their SUV struck another, stopped abruptly, and Salim and his father were crushed amongst a mangled heap of other cars.

The bus had shunted them three lanes over. The driver lay motionless with his head on the steering wheel as people rushed from their cars toward him, and several others ran toward Charlie's car.

The sky was ablaze with tiny lights from their cellphones as people were calling the emergency services. A crowd was staring at Charlie under the vehicle where she had landed, covered with blood and broken glass. Traffic was backed up behind them, and within minutes sirens screamed in the distance. People wandered dazed and numb with shock as they surveyed the carnage.

The driver of the bus was concussed and staggered from the wreck, but there was no sign of life under the car where Charlie had landed. Salim lay beneath his father's powerful body, his head, face, and arms covered with blood. No one dared touch Salim or Zayed for fear of injuring them further. No one knew if they were alive. As they waited for the emergency services to arrive it looked hopeless. But there was so much blood and twisted metal everywhere, no one could see clearly.

A paramedic team arrived by helicopter. The crew pulled Salim and Zayed from the wreckage.

Zayed was pronounced dead and Salim was immediately assessed as in a critical condition. They inserted a breathing tube before they left the scene and airlifted him to a hospital in Montpellier with life-threatening head injuries. More paramedics and emergency services arrived, including an ambulance, sirens shrieking and lights flashing.

They removed Charlie and Zayed's body from the scene. It was hours before traffic began moving again. In total, two people were dead, and eight people had been injured but none severely except Salim. The police and paramedics had said Zayed had died instantly when his skull was crushed against the hard surface of the television in the backseat of the car. When Charlie was thrown through the windshield and hit the pavement, she had died on impact. It was a tragedy made less horrific by knowing death had come instantly and they hadn't suffered.

The police found a blue backpack with an image of Simba from the movie The Lion King, and a soft toy of Simba too, on the floor of the car. The backpack had a name badge with Salim's name on it, and Charlie's purse with her driver's license was crushed in the front passenger seat, together with her cellphone. The screen was shattered but they could still see the picture of Charlie, Zayed, and Salim smiling on the home-screen.

Charlie and Zayed were taken to the morgue by the police. There was nothing in Charlie's purse or Zayed's wallet listing next of kin or who to notify in an accident. All they knew, for now, were their names and that they weren't French.

The paramedics had assessed that Salim had a serious head injury, a broken arm, and probably internal injuries. The police noted that none of them had been wearing seatbelts. All the police could deduce was that Charlie hadn't seen the oncoming bus, and possibly had been on her cellphone or texting. Both were common causes of accidents and fatalities. Beyond that, they knew nothing not even whether Salim would survive the accident. It looked unlikely when they'd left the scene and flew at full speed to Montpellier Hospital.

CHAPTER ONE

"Are you trying to kill her?" Tariq na Hassir, the formidable ruler of the Kingdom of Avana, seized the animal handler's arm, forcing him to release the rope laced around the baby giraffe's neck.

"She has suffered enough trauma." Tariq dismissed the man with a fierce scowl that struck fear into enemies.

A slither of panic crept into the young man's hushed apology. "I am sorry your Excellency."

"Release the others from their cages," Tariq growled.

The man did not have to be asked twice. He knew from experience that the Sheikh's retribution for disobedience would be swift and merciless.

"You are safe from harm," Tariq said softly, stroking the baby giraffe's long neck with a gentleness that belied his strength.

"No one will ever hurt you again, Noor," he said softly, impulsively naming her as his fingertips swept through the calf 's fur. He let his long supple fingers linger a moment upon her tail. Thankfully they had saved her in time, he thought as he reached for the reins, clenching his powerful hands around the soft leather.

The rage he had first felt on hearing about the ruthless murder of the new born's mother still roared through him. Had she been executed to pay a tail dowry to the father of some money-mongering bride, he wondered? Or did some heinous person pay thousands of dollars for a wretched fly swatter?

Noor looked up and met Tariq's dark gaze. In her innocent eyes, he saw her despair, her disillusionment, her disgust with humanity. He recognised her trauma as though it was his own. Because it was.

"Humans," he said, his voice marinated with contempt. "The people you should be able to trust, the people who say they care, the people whose actions should be driven by love —the majority are driven by nothing but selfishness, deception, and lies."

Taking a bottle of milk, Tariq placed the teat to Noor's lips. The calf 's silky black lashes grazed her cheeks as she gazed down at the foreign object then looked back at Tariq. She stared silently up at him, her eyes moist and bewildered.

Tariq had trained himself to shut down his emotions but that skill suddenly failed him. His chest trembled with suppressed rage knowing the orphaned baby would never again taste her mother's milk.

"What passes for love among some people is abhorrent," he said in a low, strained voice. "On behalf of humanity, I apologise."

The killing of the calf 's mother and three other rare Kordofan giraffes by trophy hunters seeking their tails further motivated the Sheikh's commitment to transform his anger into action.

"Do you really think you can save her?"

Tariq looked at Anwar, his younger brother by 11 months. His head was slightly bowed but he could see his eyes were fixed in sadness and longing.

Tension ripped down Tariq's spine. "Our father's reign of terror and tyranny have robbed Avana of prosperity and peace. I will make it my personal mission to right the injustices of the past. War and hostility must end. And it starts with how we treat those most vulnerable."

His fingers shook as he gripped the bottle of milk as Noor, at last, began to suckle.

An eerie silence swept across the precipitous landscape of Avana's Tiwa oasis. Tariq lifted his gaze to the horizon. The only movement visible to his naked eye was the wind etching a delicate furrow as it crawled over the golden dunes.

"Not only will I provide a sanctuary for hunted wildlife and orphans like Noor, but I will liberate God's most precious creatures from the many closing zoos and other inhumane habitats around the world," he said as he glanced over at the other animals being unloaded from the custom-built crates.

"I will create a world-acclaimed sanctuary, impenetrable by those with impure and malicious hearts. It will be the most magical, marvellous, mesmerisingly unique place, the number one eco-tourism destination in the world. I will create meaningful employment for our people, restoring their dignity, attracting millions of visitors annually and contributing billions to the economy. But more importantly, I will show the world how kindness and compassion can be turned into plutonium and change the world."

Anwar glanced at the now lush landscape and recalled how barren it had once been. With no sign of life in sight, others had found it impossible to fathom his brother's vision to transform the punishing and unforgiving conditions into a haven for so many endangered species. Yet, as with everything Tariq turned his formidable will and mind-blowing wealth to, he had succeeded where mere mortals were destined to fail.

Anwar's heart swelled with pride as he thought of all his brother's achievements. "It's an audacious and admirable plan. And if anyone can pull it off it's you, brother. Your passion, your drive, your unrelenting ambition and pursuit of goals exceeds mere mortals. And you have the endurance and power of 13,000 Arabian horses, but aren't you setting yourself up for too much hard work? Why don't you relax? Kick back. Enjoy the fruits of your reign?" Anwar said, tossing his head in the direction of the harem. "Other men would."

"Women were our father's weakness," bitterness bled from Tariq's words. "I too once made the same mistake. I too paid the price."

There was a tense silence while Tariq lifted his gaze to the sky and studied the giant falcon circling above.

"Was it not you who once taught that your greatest weakness can also be your greatest strength?" Anwar asked.

Tariq shook his head, biting down a terse retort. "I was misled," he said. He nodded his command to the animal handler lingering at a respectful distance and petted Noor as she was led away.

"All kinds of atrocities are committed in the name of love, which is why it is the most dangerous of emotions, and why I am forever turned off to women."

CHAPTER TWO

Shielding his eyes from the blazing sun, Tariq looked skyward, honing in on the falcon's intense, focused gaze. The power, the force, the courage and the vision of the hunting dog of the sky inspired him. And unlike humans falcons were loyal—a quality Tariq valued above all else.

"The best time for a man is the time he spends with his family," he said, glancing toward his brother. "My people are my family. My animals are my family. You are my family," he said, patting his brother's shoulders.

"The first responsibility of a leader is to make his people happy and then to provide them with the required security, stability, comfort, progress and development to ensure their survival. My loyalty is to you all."

Tariq's head jerked backward sharply as he recalled the brutal tyranny of his father. "Besides what sort of man doesn't want to care for his family? Only an ego-driven tyrant like our father would turn a blind eye to the plight of our people and the cruelty imposed on God's creatures."

Tariq gritted his teeth, his jaw locking against the strain of suppressing his emotions. There was no point voicing the hostility he felt toward his father. There was no purpose in reminding his brother that his father was a behemoth, a beast, a toxic mix of oppressiveness and evilness who had wielded monstrous power and made their lives a misery.

"This has to be the most isolated place in the world," Anwar muttered, gazing out forlornly at the neutrals and as-far-as-the-eye-can-see block tones of the desert. "No wonder mother fled to London."

While Tariq missed his mother deeply he didn't share his brother's despair. He was a thirty-six-year-old ruler who was pouring his power, his infinite wealth, his heart and soul into the land and the animals who he now offered sanctuary. He was a king filled with purpose.

"There is a lot of anti-Islamic sentiment in the world. People believe we are a nation of murderers. Thanks to people who corrupt our ways for their evil agenda. Thanks to our father and his violent, corrupt rule. Thanks to warlords and governments who seek to profit from war and spread their lies. Because of all these things the international community fears us. They have been driven away. I want to bring people back here. I want to restore our nation's pride. I want to show the world the beauty and kindness of true Islam. Our people have suffered enough shaming and violence," Tariq said.

"Again, you have set yourself a formidable task. Are you sure you're not throwing yourself into this audacious cause just to forget about your disobedient wife?" Anwar said.

"My ex-wife," Tariq corrected. His brief marriage had been a disaster. He should have resisted the arrangement. He should have refused to cement his father's power-base by marrying the daughter of his pugnacious uncle.

Loyalty. That was Tariq's weakness. Loyalty, to family, no matter the personal cost.

The marriage was as archaic as it was disastrous. But that didn't stop Tariq wanting a family—one that didn't place demands on him he wasn't equipped to keep.

Duty—that's what counted.

The irony didn't escape him. Duty had claimed his marriage. He knew Fatima took other lovers, just like he knew that some people weren't suited to marriage. But he also knew that if he hadn't been more married to his people and his quest than he'd ever been to his wife, he might have prevented her from escaping in the night with his bodyguard in a run-down-old jeep. He might have prevented her from being buried in the sandstorm that led to her death.

He gazed out at the stark, undulating desert landscape. If he had to atone for his sins, he'd rather do it out here where there was nothing but the eerie silence and the hot wind surfing over the dunes. Where there was nothing other than his rescued wildlife meandering over what felt like the plains of the Serengeti. Where there was nothing but the blazing desert, the sand beneath his toes, and the endless Arabian sea cutting them off from the world.

Duty required sacrifice.

Tension knotted his gut as his mind drifted to the woman who angered him most. *Melanie Jones.* It had been her fault his older brother Zayed had abdicated, and Tariq had been catapulted into the role of ruler.

Tariq vowed long ago that while he loved his older brother dearly, his disloyalty had cost too high a price. He had vowed, no matter how painful, he would never speak or think of him again.

Tariq ran his fingers down the dark brown back feathers

of the hawk. “He who wants to advance should always look ahead,” he said, turning to his younger brother.

“There are worse things than an eternity spent in this beautiful kingdom of islands, miles away from anything, draped in wind and quiet, sandstorms and hot desert breezes. Anchored between the majestic desert and surrounded by the shimmering Arabian sea. You will understand the preciousness of this gift soon enough, Anwar.”

The Kingdom of Avana had been the crown in the jewel of Tariq’s ancestors since time began. Only this time, under his rule, instead of bloody and catastrophic wars provoked by his father’s oppressive regime, the Kingdom of Avana would enjoy a reign of prosperous peace.

And he’d dedicate himself to his cause—and none other. Because when he looked around Tariq didn’t see the life-sentence his younger brother Anwar imagined, or the choke-hold his older brother Zayed had felt.

He saw his home.

Yet, while he wasn’t given to despair he could see his future as well as anyone if he continued alone. Today’s reclusive hermit is tomorrow’s bitter, old relic, Tariq told himself as the falcon left his arm and flew toward the object of his ardent desire.

He watched as the giant bird of prey courted a female falcon with acrobatic displays of daring aerial feats, Tariq was acutely aware that a kingdom wasn’t a kingdom with only a king to rule. To avoid Avana falling into the clutches of his father’s tyrannical offspring he needed an heir.

The possibility was as outrageous as it was urgent. To bear an heir he needed a wife. The whole idea was impossible. Once betrayed, a thousand times wiser, he reminded himself.

His dark brows curved into a frown as he saw his bodyguard gallop on horseback away from the towering walls of the palace toward him.

His body tensed with the stillness of a wild animal whose every sense was alert, suspicious and wary as he approached.

"Your Excellency! Come quickly. There's been an accident."

CHAPTER THREE

"Please, please, please choose me," Melanie Jones prayed inwardly. She swallowed hard, an ache building in her chest, as she checked her watch, then checked again as she paced the floor outside the Council administrative offices in central London. She heaved a deep breath as her thoughts raced.

Six minutes until her fate would be decided. She checked her watch again. Five minutes, 59 seconds until the officials from The Council, and the other key teams assessing her architectural design for the new community library, would decide her fate.

Had she done a good enough job to convince them to sign off her concept for the project? The newly elected bureaucrats in the state government had challenged her design and costings, and the whole concept was in danger of coming to a crashing end.

Had she conceded too much when she yielded to their demands to rein in her vision?

Just for once she wished she could shrug off the stigma

that dogged her when time after time, despite her award-winning designs, none of her buildings were ever constructed.

Just once she wished the vision she saw, the beauty she visualised, the joy she knew would be felt by those who eventually inhabited her buildings, was shared by those with access to the vault of money needed to bring her designs into reality.

If she could just get the dammed bureaucrats to say ‘yes’. Until then she’d be nothing but a paper architect. Her life’s work nothing but drawings and dreams.

Dreams.

Melanie rubbed her temple, erasing the one dream she had promised herself to forsake. *She was not going to think of him.*

Her ebony-black brows knitted in a fierce line as she forced her mind to the task at hand. She glanced down at the scatter of sketches splayed across the boardroom desk, feeling a mix of awe and pride—and aloneness.

Despite the fact that her design was breath stompingly beautiful, and searingly exquisite, her concept was also daringly innovative. The sweeping feminine curves confronted many people’s sense of what architecture was and what it wasn’t.

While she did everything in her power to minimize her own feminineness, in her designs aggressive masculine lines, straight edges and harsh corners were resolutely banished.

Dispelled were the sharp, angular lines and boxy shapes that so many in her field admired for their cost efficiencies. Eradicated were the shapes and forms that looked more like watchtowers in the worst of the concentration camps. Welcomed were the soaring sweeps and sensuous curves that inspired and nurtured and united people regardless of race, gender, or belief.

Melanie slid her palms over the stiff folds of her shapeless noir-black upside-down jacket. The touch of tarpaulin did an adequate job of disguising her generous breasts, but even this wouldn't detract from what many considered to be her biggest failing.

She was a woman. A woman competing in a man's world.

People, she knew only too painfully, didn't like breaking with tradition. And they didn't like change. And they most definitely didn't like a woman telling them what to do.

Everyone had told her that convincing these officials, as with all other decision-makers she had to influence, would take more than skill and strength of purpose. She was the outsider, just as her buildings were. On the edge, confronting other people's notions of compliance, and predictability, and subservience.

She'd stayed late at her office working through the night as she always did. She was quietly confident, but it was an audacious design. Why couldn't she do what her mother had always told her to do? Why couldn't she settle for less?

The community library was the biggest project she and her small team of fledgling architects had ever handled—and the most important. Books changed lives. Books made people better citizens. Books liberated people from their constrained lives.

Liberation. Freedom. Escape. She owed it to people. Her architecture was designed for everyday men and women—not the elite.

She had worked on the concept tirelessly, sacrificing the rest of her life. Architecture was her big love. *Her only love.* Work kept her guilt, and her anger, and her shame at bay, she told herself, ignoring the emptiness and longing that slopped in her belly, calling her a liar.

CHAPTER FOUR

She sucked in a breath and swept her hands brusquely across the meticulously rendered span of her designs. What she needed was an uber-rich benefactor. Someone who knew the true value of architecture. Someone who wasn't obsessed with cost concerns. Someone who knew that beauty was the hand of God creating love marks upon a world at risk of falling prey to ugliness and toxic meaninglessness.

Tariq.

Why did the thought of sky-scraping wealth and high-rise sophistication always remind her of *him*?

Because Sheikh Tariq na Hassir, the imposing ruler of the Kingdom of Avana, was almost certainly the richest man in the stratosphere. That's why.

That's the only reason you think of him, Melanie told herself firmly. Not because you're deluded enough to think he ever dreams of you and the intimacy you'd once shared. Not because you're naive enough to think he cares about you. Not because you're stupid enough to think he would ever forgive you.

Suddenly, without warning anger exploded in her chest. Why did she blame herself? Why couldn't she stop feeling that everything was always her fault? Why the hell couldn't she just forget him?

You know why.

She pressed her hand to her belly and held it there, feeling the emptiness and longing. She'd done the right thing. The only thing. It was better for everyone this way.

Wasn't it?

Doubt crawled the walls of her gut. She glanced toward the closed oak-panelled door willing it to open so she could get on with her presentation, escape into her work, erase the past, fast forward the rest of her life and quit her wishful self-indulgent wonderings.

Melanie's cell rang, distracting her from her bleak thoughts. She slid her arm into her jacket pocket, pulled it out, and lifted the phone to her ear.

"Jones," she said, sweeping her sketches into a pile with her free hand. She scanned the room to ensure she had everything she needed for her presentation.

There was a long, disquieting silence before the caller finally spoke. "Lani."

She dropped the phone to her side. Her heart squeezed tight, fisting against the sides of her chest, as the sound of the deeply familiar voice washed through her.

"It's Tariq. Tariq na Hassir," continued the deep, sultry accent.

Over three years had passed since she'd spoken to him, but Melanie knew who it was before he said his name. Her sweetheart. Her first love. The man she had cherished through university.

The man she would never allow herself to love again.

Memories of that hurt, that time when he'd abandoned

her, crowded in, pushing past the barriers she'd erected to keep her pain away.

"It's Charlotte—"

"Charlie? What's she done now?" Melanie steeled herself for what she knew could only be words of condemnation, knowing as she did that Tariq blamed her and her sister for forcing the abdication of his older brother from the sheikhdom's throne.

"She's—" A rare display of emotion brought a tremble to his normally controlled and measured voice.

Melanie's heart lurched. "What about her?"

"There's no way to break the news gently." His somber tone stilled her, summoning a pounding to her chest. "I thought I should be the one to tell you."

Panic wormed through her gut.

"She's dead."

Melanie made a strange startled sound and pressed her hand to her mouth. She sank into a chair and watched as her drawings crashed across the hard tiled floor.

"Charlotte and Zayed. They were in Paris. The car crossed the centre line. Your sister was driving," his voice barely masked the taint of blame.

"Oh, my god," she cradled her head in her arms. "Your brother? Charlie? Both dead?"

"They died instantly."

She felt a punch to her womb. *Oh, my god…the baby!* "Salim. Where is Salim?" she said, forcing the fear from her voice.

"Salim is alive."

Her heart clutched tight. "Where is he? What can I do?" Her voice was a quaver. "This is horrible." Pulse-pounding through her body she looked toward the closed door, then at her watch again. Why she didn't know. Whatever the time was she wouldn't be pitching her concept. Not today. The fact was she had to leave, and now.

Surely, they'd understand. Anyone with a heart would understand. Pulling out of the project had the potential to totally decimate her career but if she was needed now, there was no contest.

Melanie's heart thundered with pain and longing as she allowed herself to think the words she'd forced herself to deny.

Her son.

Her baby an orphan in the eyes of the law. A baby, legally speaking, with no parents. Except she was the only one who knew this was a lie.

She'd allowed her sister and Zayed to adopt him, knowing how much they wanted a child, knowing they could never bear children of their own, knowing how much her sister longed to be a mother. They could give her baby the life she could never provide.

And now they were dead.

She pushed back from the table and swept the drawings from the floor. Her hands shook as her fingers gripped the edges of the parchment. She furled her designs into a compact roll and shoved them into a telescopic drawing tube.

Her relationship with Tariq was already doomed by deception, she thought as she slung the strap over her shoulder. Salim's life was at peril. Could she finally make right the wrongs of her shameful past?

CHAPTER FIVE

Three hours later Melanie was wheeling her carry-on suitcase through the stark grey, soulless walls of Paris's Hôpital Necker when she caught sight of Tariq na Hassir. *Sheikh Tariq na Hassir*, she corrected as she took an abrupt step back, panic shooting through her in a splintering surge of shock.

She froze as he feasted his dark contemptuous gaze on her, too stunned to believe that he was really there. Too overwhelmed to comprehend that in the midst of this tragedy the man she had once loved with all her soul stood before her. Too appalled that the man who had broken her heart, the man she had believed, hoped, and prayed she would never see again was advancing toward her.

It was beyond horrific. The worst of circumstances. She wanted to flee from the tainted memories that united them and stained their past. She wanted to run from the contamination of the choices she had made. She wanted to bolt from the danger he presented but her black ankle boots felt glued to the sanitised linoleum floor.

"What are you doing here?" she hurtled out.

“I am claiming my brother’s son,” he said with righteous arrogance.

“You?” Her voice rose beyond the bounds of what was acceptable in a hospital. “You never wanted a child, isn't that what you said when you threw me from your bed?”

“You left.”

“You gave me no choice. I wanted marriage, a man who would love me—children. You didn’t. *Not with a commoner*,” Melanie said without making eye contact, her voice trembling with hurt and regret.

Tariq crossed his arms over his powerful chest. “I never said that."

“You made that abundantly clear. I wanted to be your wife—not your convenient mistress,” she gritted. “I wasn't good enough. Just like little Salim. Only he'll be worse, won't he? Salim’s a half-caste— your brother’s royal blood tainted by a Western whore. That’s what your father called my sister, didn’t he?” she fired at him. “But he was wrong. Zayed loved my sister. He married her against your father’s wishes. She was his lawful wife, not his *shameful* wench.”

I feel nothing for you, she lied to herself as she pushed past Tariq and walked toward the glass wall separating her from her son.

"Oh my god," Melanie bit her lip, blinking back tears, as she looked at the small boy lying bandaged in the paediatric hospital bed. Her fingers trembled with longing, wanting to hold her son for the first time in her arms.

Why does love always cause pain, she thought, looking up at Tariq and then back toward her son? She studied Salim’s closed eyes, his dark lashes resting peacefully against his cheeks, his wild curly hair splayed upon the starched hospital linen, his cupid lips curved into a mercifully comatose dream, she was suddenly struck by how like Tariq he was.

God, we created something beautiful.

“Where are the doctors? Nurses? Why isn't anyone here….?" She said, spinning around.

"They're preparing to leave." He said, exuding authority and a compelling magnetism that sent her pulse soaring.

"Leave? I don’t understand? Why? Where?” She stammered.

"I’m taking my brother’s child back to Avana."

“*Salim*, his name is Salim. God, can't you even say his name.”

"You’re upset."

"Yes, I'm upset," she flew at him. "My sister is dead, and now you want to take away my…” she swallowed hard, forcing back the truth she yearned to speak, “—my only connection to her."

Just like you always remove the things most important to me.

“Besides, you can't just take a three-year-old boy who has just survived a fatal car crash from the hospital.”

"I can and I will."

"He’ll die." How could she trust him, when he had deceived her before?

"Salim will die if he stays in France," he said jabbing at the headlines in a newspaper laying on the waiting room table. “The place is almost prehistoric. *Hospital fire kills*. Read it for yourself."

Melanie scanned the paper and read the article out loud, “A fire at a Paris hospital has killed eleven newborn babies. The blaze is believed to have been caused by electrical wiring.”

Her hand flew to her mouth. “How horrible…Oh my

God…Those poor babies… Those mothers… " her voice trailed off. *Mother. She was a mother.* It still didn't seem real.

"It is already decided. Only I can ensure the child's protection." Not a muscle in Tariq's hard, handsome face moved, and feeling as though he'd slapped her, as though he too considered her unworthy of the title, Melanie looked away.

"My aids have assembled and flown to my kingdom the most skilled medical staff in the world. Everything has been arranged. We leave in my private jet today."

"You can't just take my—" she paused, frantically scrambling for the right words. How could she possibly reveal the truth? His wrath would be merciless. Her deception would only make his resolve to claim her child stronger.

"You can't just take *my sister's* child like that. You have no more claim to him than I do. What about what I want?"

"You?" he almost spat the word. "Your sister murdered my brother."

CHAPTER SIX

"You can't be serious?" Tariq growled. "Your sister was untrustworthy. She beguiled him; bedazzled him; bewitched him. She drove him to distraction and then drove him to his death. If *you* hadn't introduced Charlotte to my brother, he never would have been in that damned car."

"No! It was an accident. I won't listen to that. She loved him," Melanie said. *Just like I loved you.*

"No matter what happened, no matter what passed between us, that child is mine now," Tariq said with resolute finality. "I will look after him. You have my word."

"*Your word*?" Melanie said, tearing her eyes away from her sleeping son. "Excuse me, if I don't place the same value on your promises as those you rule."

"My word is law. You will obey."

"*Obey*?" she said. "Newsflash. You're in the West now, Tariq. It's a democracy."

"I was trained to seize control and hold it," he thundered.

Her hands curled into fists on her thighs. "I will care for this child." Melanie challenged, imbuing her voice with what she hoped came across as a fierce conviction that she would be able to provide for her son. Of course, she could. *Somehow*.

She'd just walked out on the most important presentation of her career. All her other projects had come to screeching, career-stopping halts. Work had dried up. And even when things rebounded, it was impossible to have it all—a lucrative career, flourishing health, an Instagram-worthy picture of solo motherhood.

She raked her hands through her hair. What the hell was she going to do? Somehow, she had to make right the wrongs of her past.

Somehow, she had to atone for her sins. Somehow, she had to break the cycle of maternal abandonment that she had suffered as a child—no matter how unworthy or unfit she felt to be a mother.

"Salim will come home with me," she said, forcefully. "I'd rather die a tortured death than let my—my sister's child be raised by a man as cold, as stiff, as unfeeling as alloy panels. My architecture has more heart than you."

Melanie drew a ragged breath. "Salim needs love." Hadn't to be loved been all she'd ever wanted from her mother? Hadn't love been all she'd ever wanted for her son? Hadn't love been all she ever wanted from Tariq?

Love that she could trust would last a lifetime.

But no, he had broken her trust. She was a Jones, her name as common as Chins in a Chinese phone directory. Sheikh Tariq na Hassir, Sultan of the Kingdom of Avana didn't do common. And he didn't do love. Not with the under-class. And certainly not with the mother of his bastard child.

Tariq's stoic face blanched. "I will cede one thing—for the child's sake."

"And that is?" Melanie said.

"The child needs a mother's love. While your sister is gone, fortunately in appearance and not temperament, you are similar. You will be familiar to the boy. You will accompany us back to the Kingdom of Avana."

Melanie felt her heart muscles tense and then relax—the push-pull of desire and fear, the tensing of her shoulders as she fought the familiar fear of loss, betrayal, and abandonment.

Exhausted by the shock of her sister's death, strangely comforted by the knowledge that Tariq wanted to protect her son, bewildered by the knowledge that they were to be united as a family Melanie felt the safest and most afraid she had ever felt in her life.

Suddenly she couldn't keep her anger directed at him any longer. Suddenly she felt what she didn't want to feel. The desperation that she might lose her son again. She didn't want him to see her weaken. She kept her back turned to Tariq as long as possible, shielding herself from the explosive effects of his potent charisma.

It was disconcerting that just being in the same room with him sent a skyrocket of sparks tingling through her, awakening the dangerous sense of excitement and anticipation that had once seduced her into his bed.

He was so incredibly handsome it hurt to look directly at him. In the reflection of the glass, she could see his formidable black brows, the mesmerising amber golden eyes, the distinctly impervious blade of his nose.

She saw the high chiseled cheekbones, the bronze Arabic skin, the beautiful, sensual mouth that made kissing him an indescribable pleasure. She could see it all, and she wanted none of him, she lied to herself.

"You're angry," Tariq said, breaking the tense silence that gripped them both.

"I'm entitled to be. Three years ago, you dumped me. You might have told me you were always betrothed to another woman," Melanie tried to keep the wounded tone from her voice. She pressed her lips into a firm line, frustrated that it could still hurt to speak of his betrayal.

A wave of sadness slopped against her gut. There was no escaping the demeaning truth that she had been attractive enough to sleep with but not good enough to be considered for anything more important or enduring in Tariq's life.

"We have no reason to have anything to do with each other anymore!" Melanie said.

Tariq breathed in a raw-edged undertone. "I disagree," he said, glancing toward the child. "You never stayed in touch."

"Why is that your business?"

"You made it my business when you left without an explanation."

CHAPTER SEVEN

Melanie finally spun around and collided dangerously with stunning deep-set golden eyes, heavily fringed with black lashes. She felt her eyes blaze with a conflicting fire of hurt and desire and longing.

"You're in pain. We both are. Contrary to what you believe, I never stopped loving my brother. I never wished either of them dead." Tariq gazed steadily back at her, providing strength where she had none. His tension and restraint mirrored her own, both of them fighting emotions they dare not express.

Melanie turned back toward the crib where her son lay. She wanted to break through the glass, to hold in her aching arms the child she had never held, the child she had fought to shove from her consciousness, the child she had tried not to love.

The longing, the need, the shame quaked through her chest in a chaotic tempest of emotion. How much more could she take? She the battler, the fighter, the warrior…how much more could she fake?

How much longer could she pretend she didn't care?

"Oh, Tariq, this is just awful."

He moved toward her, and reached for her hand, and squeezed it as he said, "Everything will be alright."

His touch and words of reassurance seared through her grief. She was suddenly aware of every ragged breath she took the irregular bump of her heart, and the blazing heat of his body.

She moved away from him so that his hand fell from hers. She shouldn't be feeling anything for him. She should be feeling grief, and anger, and pain.

Yet she yearned for the comfort she had once felt in his powerful arms. She wanted desperately to believe that everything would be alright.

She rubbed her hands together, trying to dislodge the lingering tingle of awareness. Suddenly he scooped her into his all-powerful arms. In shock, as a frisson of pleasure scuttled through her body, Melanie stopped breathing. She hated him, despised him, she told herself, hopelessly striving for her usual objectivity.

He betrayed me.

She shouldn't be feeling the traitorous zing of desire, she thought with relentless logic.

"Don't," she protested breathlessly, sinking into his warm protective embrace. Nothing had changed. If anything, distance and time apart had only made their chemistry grow stronger. For the first time in years, she actually felt supported.

"Right now, all we have to get us through this ordeal is each other. You and I," Tariq husked, reaching up to grasp her chin, "We once comforted each other very successfully—"

"Successful to you means something vastly different than

successful does to me," Melanie rebuked, her body trembling. "I feel like a failure."

She swallowed, feeling herself choke up, then turned to him with all the fierceness she could summon. "Correction. I *felt* like a failure. I'm over you."

"You were unforgettable," Tariq whispered, not believing her for a moment. "I've never forgotten our first kiss." His eyes, the colour of a desert moonlight, connected with hers, gleaming with dark desire.

Melanie tried to wrestle free but when his kiss came it claimed her mercilessly. The almost forgotten scent of him assailed her senses: the melody of cinnamon and Arabic spices so intoxicatingly familiar she was instantly transported to that first night three years earlier when he had first claimed her as his own. "No. Tariq. Not like this. Not now. *Not ever.*"

His hot, urgent mouth went down on hers and he feasted on her protesting lips with passionate determination, plundering and ravishing with a thrilling ability to ignite her own dormant hunger.

Exquisite excitement shook through Melanie like a thunderbolt igniting every neuron in her body. The erotic thrust of his probing tongue into her mouth consumed her with a burning desire and a crazy urge to draw even closer to his lean, virile body.

Wild hunger started a throb of warmth in her pelvis and made her nipples harden. She wanted him, she wanted them, she wanted the dream. Him, her, their son.

She wanted a happy family.

And then sanity returned like a bucket of ice on her overheated skin when her thoughts drifted to Salim, jarring every maternal sense she never thought she possessed back to wakefulness.

What if Tariq discovered the truth? What if he learned of

her deception? What if it was true—she was irrevocably flawed?

Three years ago, Tariq had made his choice abundantly clear. She had been jilted mercilessly. Instead he had married a virtual stranger. A woman with royal blood coursing through her veins. Someone as aristocratic, sophisticated, and regal as he was. Not someone with a tainted past.

Wrenching her mouth free of his lips, Melanie looked up into the smouldering dark golden eyes that had once broken her heart. And she said what she needed to say, what she owed it to herself to say.

"Please leave us Tariq. Let me take my—my *sister's* baby."

CHAPTER EIGHT

"Is he not magnificent?" Tariq lifted his powerful arm as he strode through the cabin of his private jet toward her.

"As far as large, *very large*, birds go," Melanie said, white-knuckling the armrest, as she studied the falcon's sharp claws, the even sharper beak of the bird perched possessively on Tariq's wrist, "I am sure he is very handsome."

Every bit as handsome and as unpredictable, and as dangerous as you, she thought as she watched Tariq place the giant bird of prey into his own purpose-built restraint.

She should have been annoyed by the tenderness Tariq showed the injured creature but she was glad he was distracted. With any luck, he would maintain his focus on his feathered friend and far away from Salim who was being cared for in the back of the aircraft.

She lifted her hand to her chest and fingered the locket which rested on her heart, hidden beneath the high neckline of her black tunic. Inside the locket was the only picture she had of her son, taken on the morning she gave him up and entrusted him into her sister's care, and fine strands of his ebony black baby hair. She heaved a sigh of relief grateful that Tariq had not noticed the undeniable likeness to him that their son possessed.

"Does your good-looking friend have a name?" she asked, forcing herself to show enthusiasm. Tariq seemed to be more concerned about the bird than the injured boy who was his son. But of course, he didn't know that. *Would never know that.* Not until she could be sure he would not claim his son upon learning the truth and banish her from the kingdom and Salim's life forever.

"His name is *Maqdira*," Tariq said. "It means strength, ability, and potency," he said looking at her intensely.

Tariq's gaze made her body flush with heat. She lowered her eyes to his powerful hands, but they offered no respite from the unwanted feelings that coursed through her body. She felt her stomach curl. Everything inside her felt twisted and heated.

But given the affection and reverence he gave the bird it seemed he was oblivious to the powerful effect he was having on her. Other than assuming the role of protecting Salim he had not shown the boy one drop of kindness. Instead, quite the opposite. It was almost as though he found it easier to pour love on an animal, she thought with annoyance. Was he incapable of showing their child the same tenderness?

"*Maqdira* has a passport, travels first-class and has his own seat on the plane—anyone would think he was human," Melanie said, noticing with alarm the wounded, childish tone to her voice. Was she jealous of a bird?

Tariq's black eyes swept her face with disturbing intensity.

You care more for him than me. You care more for him than our son. Her mind drifted to Salim and the difficulties which lay ahead for them all, not least of which was worrying how Tariq would react when at last she found the right time to tell him the truth.

Melanie opened her mouth then closed it again because she knew one wrong word, one wounded sentence, one uncensored word and she would betray the secret she knew she must keep.

Tariq checked the bird once again and then turned toward the cockpit.

"Where are you going?"

"The plane won't fly itself."

"You're going to fly this thing?"

"I can assure you that you will be perfectly safe."

His tone of supreme confidence reassured her. Of course, he'd fly his own plane. Nothing Tariq did was left to chance. Everything had to be controlled.

"How long is the flight from Paris to Avana?"

"7 hours and 45 minutes," Tariq said.

Melanie slid back and settled into the plush cream leather seat, glad of the opportunity to have some time to herself to figure out what she was going to do and say when they landed in Avana.

Had it not been for his fierce-looking bird of prey, as she watched Tariq stride away from her she should have felt relieved to have been spared his company and with it the likelihood she would blurt something out she'd later regret.

As the plane taxied, *Maqdira* narrowed its gaze and pinned her with a distinctly unfriendly stare. It was almost as though it looked right through her soul and saw her deception.

"You think you know me, but you don't," she whispered to the bird. "How can you? I don't even know myself."

The falcon leaned forward as though assessing her.

"I get it," she said, "You're loyal. I admire that." *He loves you. I want that.*

God, what am I doing talking to a bird, she thought as she turned and looked out the window? She felt her stomach clench as the plane lifted off.

Goodbye, she said inwardly, wondering what lay ahead. The only thing she knew for certain was she couldn't escape the feeling of dread which wormed through her gut.

Would Tariq's people welcome her? Would they accept a foreigner? Or would she be met with suspicion? Or worst, would the blame of Tariq's kingdom assail her the moment she stepped off the plane? She knew with gut-clenching clarity she would be the outsider, the stranger, the unknown threat.

She glanced at *Maqdira* who stood stoically regarding her, his gaze unflinching, his pose ruthlessly asserting his loyalty.

Somehow she had to rise above it all—whatever happened, somehow she had to summon the strength and the determination to emerge victoriously.

CHAPTER NINE

Soaring above the clouds as he approached the Kingdom of Avana Tariq could see things from a higher perspective. Melanie had come crashing into his life for a reason. Maybe it was finally payback time, Tariq reflected grimly, as he guided the plane past the familiar mountains covered in fragrant frankincense trees.

He traced his tongue across his lips and tasted the scent of their illicit hospital kiss as the jet soared over the red rocks and historic caves toward the azure waters of the Arabian Sea. His brows knotted with concern as he noticed his body swim with swollen desire.

The truth was he had once made a commitment to her that he wasn't free to keep. His commitment had not been given verbally, but spiritually. His heart had been drawn to her the first time he had laid eyes on her. He gripped the throttle and steered the plane toward the final stage of their flight.

He should've been stronger. Bedding her all those years ago had been a mistake. A moment of weakness had led him to her bed again after all those years apart. He'd been shocked at seeing her in the unfamiliar circumstances of a design symposium for Arab leaders. She had looked just as alluring as she had when they were in college together.

He wasn't free to choose. Not then and now. His future was decided, guided, mandated by the responsibility he had for his people. He could not commit to himself. He was the ruler of the wealthiest principality in the world and yet he could not commit freely to his desires.

Not fully.

What was preventing him? Duty. Loyalty. A promise. A promise he had once made to Fatima and had failed. But the marriage was years ago. Didn't he owe it to his people to prove his damaged heart was invincible? His thoughts drifted to Melanie. Their DNA was forever entwined. She had been the first. Wasn't this why Melanie was an addiction he couldn't break?

He must remain strong. He must keep his resolve. He must maintain control he vowed as he fixed his gaze on the steel maze of different knobs, switches, and other controls in the cockpit. His brother had paid a high price for defying their late father and marrying a foreigner from a different culture.

And Melanie was to blame. It was Melanie who had introduced her sister Charlie to his brother. It was Melanie who had orchestrated that fateful relationship. It was Melanie who had tempted him with the depth of illumination that sparkled from her infinite eyes.

Tariq grabbed the throttle in a vice-like grip. He had no role for love in his life. No room in his heart for the pain of it. That was why his brother's death had no more impact than hearing about the death of a stranger on CNN.

He lifted his hand and pressed his palm to his chest and tried to ignore the clutch of his heart calling him a liar. He had built an unpenetrable fortress around the most fragile and unpredictable of organs. He had forced his heart to yield to his logical mind. Like a wilful, undisciplined Arabian horse his heart would no longer dictate his path. His heart would no longer run amok, sweeping freely across the treacherous landscape of tears.

And yet the very thought of Melanie being in his power was the most seductive image in years of tireless work for his Kingdom that Tariq had indulged.

Tariq placed a white-knuckle grip on the throttle as the airplane hit a patch of turbulence, and guided the plane's gradual descent.

An image of his beloved grandfather passed like a whisper as the plane dropped below the cloud. He had shut his heart before his grandfather's brutal murder. He had shut his heart before his father's reign of terror. He had shut his heart before his wife's betrayal. Every betrayal, every hurt, every hurtful thing that had happened had been caused by humans, he thought as at last the wide expanse of glittering, pearl laden sea edging the desert kingdom of Avana appeared beneath the horizon.

Tariq felt a surge of protective pride as a tower of giraffes sauntering across the hot sands came into view. His animals, like his subjects, loved unconditionally and loyally. They deserved his heart. No one else, he affirmed, steeling his resolve as his thoughts drifted once again to Melanie.

Since taking her to his bed that fateful night those years ago destiny seemed forever enmeshed. The unbidden kiss at the hospital had only rekindled the dangerous fire.

Think quickly and act fast, he thought as he guided the plane toward the runway. His father's voice drummed through his ears. *Seize every opportunity that you contend will benefit you in the long run.* While his relationship with his father had been fraught his maxim was one of the few things that Tariq trusted.

Too many people lacked vision, he thought, lowering the wheels. Too many people took a short-term view and allowed petty squabbles and pride to detract from the things that truly mattered. Too many people let emotion cloud their judgment.

He gripped the throttle and thrust it into neutral, firmly placing a handbrake on his dreams. As the plane taxied to a stop Tariq felt something unfurl in his chest. The truth was he was bored. Bringing Melanie to Avana and keeping her here might just add the spice his life was lacking.

Perhaps the accident, as tragic as it was would benefit him in the long run. He would protect his brother's child. He would explore the connection he still felt to Melanie. For as long as he denied the magnetic pull that fatally drew him to her he knew he would be vulnerable to her charms.

And vulnerability in a man was the most despicable of weaknesses. An Achilles heel that would ultimately lead to downfall, and Tariq, despite his formidable willpower, had just discovered his treacherous heart was no longer impenetrable.

Melanie was an addiction he couldn't break. Not yet. Immersion therapy wasn't that what behavioural psychologists advised. He thought of his friend, Massimiliano Balforni, CEO of Emporio Balforni, Milan's most prestigious fashion house, and the art therapist who had induced such a miraculous, transformational change in him.

Consume so much of something it makes you sick and at last, you are free. Forever and always. Or, so they said. A faint pulse throbbed beneath his fingertips. What did he have to lose?

CHAPTER TEN

His self-reliance. That's what he had to lose. Max, the man, who had sworn he would never marry, had made the therapist his wife!

As the plane approached the runway a haze of flashing lights and sirens refocused Tariq's thoughts. Salim had been constantly monitored by experienced doctors and nurses using the latest medical devices throughout the flight. Now it was time for the medics to take him home.

Home.

It suddenly struck Tariq how *Waardi* Palace had never felt like home. Not to humans. Certainly not to Tariq. And never for a child. He'd never spent longer than a month there before being shunted to a series of international boarding schools and military-style bastions of education fit for a king but bereft of emotional comfort and sustenance.

Since being catapulted prematurely onto the throne, Tariq had successfully distracted himself from his traumatic childhood. With determined focus and purpose, he had created a refuge for animals. How ironic that, he so incapable of caring, was now bringing a severely traumatised child back to the very place he had once banished from his heart. Tariq was an expert in caring for orphaned giraffes and other endangered species, but could he succeed in creating a refuge for an orphaned child?

Then there was Melanie.

He didn't know who would threaten his defences more. His aides would care for the boy, Salim's injuries demanded it. *But her.* How was he going to sate his physical cravings yet keep his emotional distance from the woman who had once meant so much to him?

"Will you be accompanying the boy, Your highness?" His aide asked, entering the cockpit.

Do not get too close. Do not fail this child with your inability to feel.

"Go on ahead," he said, hoping his aide didn't detect the strain in his voice, the tension in his body, the irrational fear that gripped him.

"Where are they taking him," Melanie demanded, her voice urgent as Salim was wheeled from the plane.

"My intensive care team will travel with him as he is transported with the ground ambulance for the three-hour drive to the palace. They are equipped with medical equipment to the same level as an intensive care station in a hospital," he added, answering the unspoken anxiety that played on her pallid face and pale lips.

God, she was beautiful. Melanie Jones was even more beautiful than he remembered. Although she had just suffered the incalculable pain of losing her sister and had endured a long, fraught flight, her eyes shone with light.

"My staff have prepared everything and will offer him the comfort he needs should he wake," he said, fighting the desire that surged through his limbs on a wave of thoughts and sensations.

"I should be there. I should go with him." She said, with the fierceness of a lioness protecting her cub. It was endearing he thought, how much she cared for a child that wasn't even her own. Tariq's own mother had never shown him as much affection. In fact, even before she fled to London she had been a stranger.

His eyes strayed as Melanie turned from him. Her boxy black suit couldn't hide the lithe and shapely body he'd held in his arms. The passing of the years had only made her more mesmerising, no matter how much she tried to conceal her feminine charms beneath her masculine suits and her stiff demeanour.

Tariq caught her arm as she tried to leave the plane and race after the ambulance. "There is nothing you can offer that my medics cannot do better."

"Love," she threw at him. "Love is what I can do better."

CHAPTER ELEVEN

Tariq was right, Melanie told herself reluctantly as she climbed into the backseat of the chauffeured Mercedes convertible. Salim was being cared for by some of the top medical professionals in the world. She took in her new surroundings, twisting her large onyx ring around her finger as they made their way toward the palace.

Palm trees lined the road. It was summer and they were thick with succulent dates. She watched as she saw a group of young men climbing one of the tallest trees. Tariq suddenly asked his driver to stop and back up. He saw that the men were struggling to pick the dates from the high palms.

He picked up his phone and told her he was calling his Agriculture Minister. "I don't want anyone to get hurt or tired climbing our palms," he said to his Agriculture Minister. "Start planting low palm trees so that people can eat the dates when they are needy. The taller ones can stay for decoration."

Melanie watched as Tariq got out of the convertible and beckoned to the men to come down. He handed them some money and they smiled as they expressed their appreciation at Tariq who nodded graciously, then turned back toward the car, as though the solemness of the occasion had returned with a thud.

Despite his own grief, Melanie realised Tariq feared for the life of the young men climbing his date trees. What kind of ruthless ruler does that? What kind of man does that?

"Before His Majesty, there was a lack of welfare," his driver said, with barely restrained annoyance, as though anticipating her surprised thoughts. "It was a time when those in power kept the nation's wealth for themselves and people fought for survival. Since his rule people no longer fight to stay alive. Everyone enjoys the benefits and pleasures of living well," he said, barely concealing his distrust of her motives.

It didn't escape Melanie that the driver didn't mention Tariq's father directly. Almost as though he still feared some retribution. And Melanie couldn't disagree. Everyone and everything looked prosperous. There were no beggars at the airport. No homeless people, or shantytowns, or dilapidated buildings on the drive to *Waardi*. No clear demarcation of the haves and have nots—other than of course Tariq's palace which she had yet to see.

She knew much of the flaunting of wealth was historical in origin. She knew Avana was like other countries who fought to maintain their royal families and regencies around the world. She knew many people loved the romance of a palace, the prestige, the magic.

Almost, even though they knew there were strict rules about who was worthy enough to marry a royal, as if they were clinging onto a cinderella-dream that one day someone in their family might marry a prince and become a princess. Especially to someone kind and generous and benevolent, she thought, momentarily entertaining the fantasy.

Wake up, Melanie, she censored herself. You're a Jones.

Common as toads. No Jones has ever married a prince and certainly not a woman who has conducted herself so badly.

“His Highness is an unbelievable force of nature,” the driver continued. “A powcrful soul inside a man’s body. Because of His Highness, the sleepy seaside villages surrounding Avana were turned into prosperous cities. For that reason, he will always stay in the hearts and minds of people. Already he has achieved so much during his time of rule. He fostered growth and fostered a generation of educated citizens and because of him, we have entered an enlightened time, where our ruler has the right heart, tools, and knowledge to progress the nation. With his generosity and kindness, he built this entire country with honour.”

He turned to her, his dark eyes growing black. “It was not right how his wife disrespected him. It was not right how his brother abandoned him. It was not right how he has suffered some truly despicable and treacherous and untrustworthy behaviour. We are all happy to be children of Sheikh Tariq. May Allah bless him and give him the happiness he deserves. And for those who hurt him—well, let’s just say, it would be a mistake.”

She was glad of the reprieve as Tariq returned to the car. “You care about these men, don’t you? You genuinely care, don't you?”

“Of course. These men are my sons, my people, my family. I will do everything in my power to protect them.”

"Your sons?” She said, pointing in the direction of the young men.”But they're not much younger than you.”

“Tariq is not just a leader. He is the father of this nation,” his driver said, glancing first at Tariq for approval to speak.

She noticed that when he talked about Tariq or looked at him it was always with positivity and love. And yet toward her, he showed none of the benevolence that inspired Tariq's people.

As the Mercedes continued its journey Melanie watched as a young boy drew a blade and a severed bunch of dates fell to the hard, arid ground.

Tariq may look sweet, she thought, crossing her arms over her chest as she glanced at him, but there's no telling how he will react if he ever discovered she had concealed the truth of their son from him all these years.

Perhaps he'd be happy to see her fall. Maybe he would take pleasure in causing her pain. What if by hurting him as she had, and still was by hiding his son from him, when he discovered the truth he took pleasure in adding to her already incalculable hurt? Only this time the pain would be twice as sharp. Because once he learned the truth now Tariq had the power to invoke *sharia* and use Islamic law to keep her son from her permanently.

The truth of it pummelled through her brain as they approached the fortress-like walls surrounding the palace. But knew, as the Mercedes made its approach toward the palace and she glanced at the soldiers armed with assault rifles, that a ruthless streak ran through Tariq's DNA.

She knew as everyone who made it their mission to keep an eye to world affairs, that his father had been a singularly harsh and corrupt man. She hadn't heard of any men in power, certainly not men of Tariq's descent and stature, who hadn't gained power, nor kept it, without cultivating and maintaining a formidable presence.

Horror crashed through her chest. She was now a foreigner on foreign land beyond the protection of Western law.

She never should have come. But what choice did he give her?

CHAPTER TWELVE

"Why is everyone so unfriendly?" Melanie said to Tariq, glancing at the frowning sentries as they approached the entrance.

"You are a foreigner. They think you are their enemy."

"What? They don't even know me. "

"You are a Westerner."

"Am I supposed to apologise for that?"

"Of course not. But you must understand. I will not lie to you. What you are feeling, what you are sensing is real. The contempt of my people, their fear, their anger—it is the same distrust that Muslim men and women experience when they go to your country. They think you are against them because your leaders preach hate."

"That's ridiculous. I can't be held responsible for what people I didn't even vote for think and believe." Melanie's eyes grew hot, a contrast to the cold weight crushing her lungs.

Tariq shrugged. "That is how the world is."

"I'm not anti-Muslim. Far from it. You know that more than anyone."

I love a Muslim man.

"Perhaps," he said, regarding her skeptically.

"Will I ever be accepted? If, I am to live in peace while I wait for Salim to recover they need to know I am not their enemy."

"That is up to you."

"Me?"

"Only you can prove yourself trustworthy. Unfortunately, my people have still not forgiven your sister for seducing my brother Zayed."

"And you?"

"You know what I think."

"No Tariq I don't. I never know what you think because you always hide your feelings. You're so reserved and stoic you may as well be made of the same marble tiles as those towers," she said, gesturing to the mosaic minarets, rising like steeples from the fortress-like walls marking the palace from the hot, flat land. "You're every bit as cryptic and doubly complex."

"Very well, you want to know what I think? I think you come from a family of liars."

The force of his words sent her reeling. *Did he know?*

Melanie clutched her hands to stop her fingers from shaking. Fake supreme confidence, she told herself. Make it look as though the past never happened, she told herself, averting her eyes from his probing gaze to the palace.

Her vision drifted up along the high austere walls protecting the entrance from ancient enemies and unwanted intruders, then soared toward the macho domes glaring across at each other like two heavy-weight boxers at a weigh-in.

If the atmosphere weren't so tense she would have marvelled at the awe-inspiring architectural feat and the impossibly lofty cupolas. Instead, she felt imprisoned by the weight of the secret that kept her captive.

“Everyone lies,” Melanie said brushing at her jacket, crumpled from the long journey from Paris to Avana. "Somc-times to protect people from harm, and sometimes for their own advancement." She tucked a flyaway strand of hair behind her ear and pinned her gaze on Tariq as his dark eyes locked on hers.

“Your father fed this country nothing but lies since he inherited the throne—or rather stole the throne when he over-threw his own father—your grandfather, King Hamza,” she hurled at him, continuing the duel his accusation had incited.

Tariq’s face froze, the golden bronze pallor of his skin paling in sudden shock.

“Don’t look so surprised. I do read the *Guardian,* you know. And all the other international newspapers independent of the long, gilded arm of your father’s corruption and fake-news. Your father stole the crown from your grandfather and then set about spending the Kingdom’s wealth. And, if almost forcing what was once the richest realm in the world into bankruptcy, that wasn’t enough, he set about stealing the one thing that mattered most. People’s freedom. Their liberty. And no one's liberty was stolen more than women.”

What did it matter what his father had done and what Tariq thought of her, she told herself, ignoring the tightness of her chest, the knotting of her shoulders, the dull, constant ache that drummed through her heart. She wasn’t going to stay. As soon as Salim was well she would leave. She would never, ever return. Melanie fisted her hands into her pocket. She didn’t want to fight. She wanted—no. She told herself firmly, clenching her fists as her dream of happy families coiled around her like the hot desert wind. It didn't matter what she wanted.

Tariq hadn't brought her to Avana to rekindle their on-again, off-again romance. Or had he, she wondered remembering their embrace in the hospital and the heated kiss which still scorched her lips?

Stop it, she told herself. It's all a mirage. As far as Tariq was concerned she was a stand-in mother for an unwanted child.

"Look, Tariq, this is going nowhere. I didn't come all this way to argue with you. Your father, my sister…your brother…they are all dead. And Salim is alive. He is what matters. I don't give a damn what people think of me," she said, her stomach clenching as the elaborately carved giant doors, guarded by the armed sentries, opened.

"I have spent my whole life being the outsider, my whole childhood being the girl nobody wanted, my whole youth being the woman who was never accepted. And I've spent my adulthood being the architect rejected for her sex, not her talent. I'm not going to change and I'll be damned if I will let anyone's stereotype define me. I don't like to be painted as someone I'm not. So while I wait for Salim to get well I will show your people that I am not a bigot. I will show them I'm not racist. I will show them they are wrong."

And I will prove my worth to you.

She saw his shoulders tighten as he pinned her beneath his dark, unfathomable gaze.

"Salim may be the only reason you have invited me into your inner sanctum," she said stepping inside the walls for the first time. "But I will make the most of this opportunity to immerse myself in a new culture, learn new skills, improve my mind—and you, Tariq will help me," she said, surprising herself as much as him by her demand, judging from his smile of quiet appreciation.

"How so?" he said, his eyebrows arching.

"I'm an architect. It's my passion. I would like to know more about Islamic art. I would like to become more familiar with your culture, with what inspires your people. I would like to keep my mind engaged, my thoughts busy while Salim heals." *My feelings contained,* "That is what you can do for me," she said.

"That suits me perfectly," he said, the double-meaning of his tone surprised her. Did he have some hidden agenda for her, she wondered, as the gates crawled open?

Melanie held her breath, unprepared for the shock of beauty that assailed her. "It's like entering into another world. It's—"

"Paradise," he said, finishing her words. "It's what my grandfather and our successors, strove to achieve. Heaven on earth. B*efore him*—before my father," he said with heated emotion. "My father may have renamed the palace after himself but thankfully he stopped at completely bastardising the place."

Bastard. The word assailed her. Would he think Salim was a bastard child when he found out the truth?

CHAPTER THIRTEEN

"After my father died the first thing I did was rename the palace. My Grandfather had named it *Waardi, which* can also be used to describe a lion that has black strands in its mane," Tariq said.

"The darker, fuller manes indicate a healthy lion with plenty of testosterone. Black manes are perhaps the most telling status-symbol; they darken with age, and the thick dark hair indicates a well-fed lion. That means a black-maned lion is likely in his prime, eating well, and getting plenty of loving from the ladies."

Melanie swallowed hard, trying to fight the crawl of nerves swarming through her body like a swarm of wasps. She rubbed her fingers over her locket which contained the black strands of hair that had crowned her son's head when he was born.

Her little lion. That's what he was. Inwardly she prayed that he too possessed the same qualities as his father. Qualities he would need to survive. Fearlessness, determination, and ferociousness.

"When my father took the throne he immediately

renamed the palace, *Abbas*," Tariq said, oblivious to her disquiet. "In Arabic, this name is given to the meanest and strongest lion in the pride! It is the lion that all others fear."

"Which explains why the entrance is so imposing," she said.

"It is designed to strike fear into enemies from the outside but inside the original vision and design aesthetic of my ancestors has largely remained untouched. As you will discover, the deeper you journey into the palace the more softness and sensuousness and tranquility you will find. It opens out like a flower," he said, as they reached the main courtyard which majestically marked the heart of the citadel formed by a complex of palaces, gardens, and forts.

Architecturally it was beyond impressive, it was sublime, Melanie thought, surprised that something as elaborately embellished could create such profound peace.

The oblong courtyard was surrounded by a low gallery supported on 124 white marble columns. A pavilion projected into the courtyard at each extremity, with filigree walls and a light domed roof, all elaborately ornamented.

The square was paved with sapphire and gold-coloured tiles, and the colonnade with white marble. The walls were covered 1.5 meters up from the ground with more tiles, with a border above and below enamelled blue and gold. The whole form of piers, arches, and pillars was so graceful it almost belied its imposing strength.

"Why do you not revert back to the original name your ancestors used. What did you say? A flower?"

"I have thought about it many times. For a flower can be tender and dangerous at the same time," he said. "A ruler needs both. Hemlock can kill and the castor oil plant or Palm of Christ is more poisonous than cyanide. However, lions are significant to Arabs. Arabs love lions so much many families name their sons after them."

Melanie followed after Tariq as he walked toward a magnificent alabaster basin supported by the figures of twelve lions in white marble.

"There are no prizes for guessing why we call this the Court of Lions," he said, a rare smile lifted the corners of his formidable lips.

"Each lion has a unique quality. These are strength, power, and sovereignty," he said, his hand anointed the head of the first three lions. "These three are ferocity, endurance, and stamina. A lion must love with all his heart and last the distance. When he loves it is forever," he said, his voice a trawl of seduction.

"I call this one Bahnas, a lion that swaggers and prances while walking. You will see what I mean when you meet some of the men in my family. Hamza was my grandfather's name. He was the most enduring of the lions. The name denotes power and leadership. If your name is Dhergham then your name denotes fearlessness. More specifically it refers to a tough and fearless lion with magnificent sharp teeth!"

Melanie thought back to the time Tariq nibbled her neck, her breasts, her belly. A frisson of yearning scuttled through her. She clenched her teeth, willing the dangerous need to leave.

"And this is Adl—justice, " he said, his hand lingering on the last lion. "A lion always seeks vengeance."

Melanie swallowed hard, her throat as dry as the desert sands. What vengeance would he seek when he learned the truth of her deception?

She noticed an inscription of Arabic words trailing along the base of the fountain. "What does that say?" she asked

Tariq, steering her thoughts away from the fear of his swift justice.

“It is a poem by an ancient mystic to describe the beauty of the courtyard.”

“Will you read it to me?”

CHAPTER FOURTEEN

Tariq's brows knitted into a fierce line, then softened. Melanie followed him as he stepped toward the fountain and knelt at the base.

"Such a translucent basin, sculpted pearl," he said, reading the inscription, "Argentic ripples are added on it by the quiet dew. And its liquid silver goes over the daisies, melted, and even purer. Hard and soft are so close, that it would be hard to distinguish," he said, reading the lines she felt he already knew from heart, deliberately avoiding her glance.

"Liquid and solid, marble and water. Which one is running? Don't you see how water overflows the borders and the warned drains are here against it?"

She noticed his shoulders tighten as he hesitated.

"Go on," she encouraged.

He cleared his throat. "They are like the lover who in vain tries to hide his tears from his beloved."

He turned to Melanie his dark eyes holding hers in what Melanie instinctively felt was a moment of truthful reconciliation. All these years, when she had thought he had abandoned her, had he in fact been hiding his pain?

The sound of clapping echoed across the vast courtyard. “Bravo. Very poetic.”

Melanie blinked, shielding her eyes from the searing sun, as her gaze traveled the length of the formidable man who advanced toward her. Dressed in the typical attire of pretty much every man on the Arabian peninsula: a long white *dishdashi* that emphasised the elegance of his powerful physique.

“I thought you were in New York,” Tariq said, sharply. He ignored the man’s outstretched hand, as he rose to his feet.

“And who is this utterly beautiful woman?” the stranger said. His eyes were expressionless as he helped Melanie to her feet. He lifted her fingers to his face and pressed his lips against the back of her hand. “Hamad,” he said, “At your service,” he bowed elaborately, then rose, grinning.

“You know who she is. I sent you a text to say she was returning with my brother’s child.”

It didn’t escape Melanie’s attention that Tariq mentioned neither her name nor Salim’s nor that of her sister’s. It was as though they didn't exist.

“But you never mentioned her exquisite beauty. Why was that cousin?” Hamad provoked.

"The extravagance—I will not tolerate it. What the hell were you thinking?” Tariq said, changing the subject dramatically. 577 million dollars for a painting no one but you will ever see. It’s obscene."

Melanie forced a smile. As charming and handsome and rich as he was, she made a mental note to file Hamad under her growing list of Islamic rule breakers. Still, at least everyone wasn’t unfriendly.

“The timing of your childish flirtation is ill-considered. I’m tired and in no mood for these games, Hamad. My brother has been killed. Yet all you can think about is a grieving woman's beauty."

Beauty? Does Tariq think she is beautiful? Impossible, Charlotte was the beauty in the family, Melanie reminded herself.

Hamad pressed his lips into a hard line as though biting back a retort and lowered his head.

"Have you made the arrangements?" Tariq demanded.

"It's complicated."

"What do you mean complicated?"

"Your brother abdicated. A royal funeral is out of the question."

"I determine the rules," Tariq said, drawing himself up to his full imposing statue. "I determine what is law. What is acceptable. Who comes and who goes. Now do as I have decreed," he said, advancing toward the buggy waiting for him. Tariq gestured for Melanie to join him. He watched his cousin out of the corner of his eye and frowned as he retreated.

"Gosh, your cousin—he's—."

"Like catnip for women?"

"I didn't say that."

"You didn't have to. My cousin is known to women as the Sultan of Seduction. Just because someone is friendly and charming doesn't make them worthy of your trust," Tariq said.

"What are you trying to say?"

"Be careful. That's all. What you do with your time, who you care to give your affection to doesn't concern me. You're not expected to work and you need not worry about money."

"I'm used to making my own way in life. I can't just abandon everything—and now you're telling me who I may spend time with? What is this? A jail?"

"I do not intend to imprison you. I only ask for your discretion."

"So, it's true."

"What's true?" His wide, arrogant mouth pressed in a hard line.

"You really don't care about me, at all."

CHAPTER FIFTEEN

"Isn't it archaic, somewhat misogynic to force women to cover themselves from head to toe?" she said, as they drove through the palace grounds.

"Avana law requires women to wear decent, respectful clothing. It is for their own protection. Women are free to decide what form it should take," Tariq said. "Unlike our brothers in Iran, we have not made Islamic dress mandatory for women."

Melanie glanced down at the stiff, coarse folds of her military-style attire. Black power trouser suits were her uniform. Her protection. Her weapon of equality. She had always liked the way her clothes distracted from her appearance. Trousers were liberating. An act of rebellion.

"Besides," he added, "I don't believe the hijab or the abaya is an issue. Society has changed its views towards many things and the hijab is one of them. In fact, many women believe they stand out in a positive way, which makes them feel very special and very proud.

Melanie thought about her muse Coco Chanel and how she had pioneered the emancipation of women. Her weapon of destruction was clothes. With little more than a sewing machine she had liberated women from annoying claustrophobic, terribly trivialising and severely impractical corseted dresses.

Nonetheless, Melanie longingly admired the striking, filmy candour of delicately printed chiffon and other fabrics that enveloped Avana women of all ages and backgrounds as they moved about in public.

"If I were not afraid my work would no longer be taken seriously," she said, "I think I would happily adopt Avana's style of dress, " she said, impulsively. "It's so intensely feminine and mysteriously modest at the same time."

The women were also profoundly beautiful, she thought as she watched a middle-aged woman walk through the crowd. She held herself with poise and pride, and confidence, the only part of her skin visible were her Kohl-rimmed eyes, which could barely be seen through the slits of her hijab.

Even in the distance, she could detect the mischievous sparkle as though she was profoundly aware of her beauty but thankful also for the mystery and protection her garments gave her from strangers and the unwanted advances of men. Wasn't that what Melanie also sought to achieve from her power suits—protection, equality, and freedom?

She ran her fingers under the waistband of her trousers and tugged the coarse fabric away from her hips and belly. If she were truly honest, wearing trousers was every bit as restrictive as a corseted dress. Especially in this oppressive heat.

"That was a big sigh," Tariq said.

"It's so unbearably hot and sticky here," she said, aware Tariq's eyes were following the line of her fingers as she reached beneath her blouse and ran her palm across the pooling beads of sweat. "What temperature is it?"

"Avana is spread along the coastline of the Arabian Gulf and that summer sun brings very high humidity. Temperatures can reach 45 °C (113 °F) for many days. Even the sea temperature reaches 37 °C (99 °F).

"Does it ever cool down?"

"If you stay long enough you'll experience sandstorms, rain and even snow," he said.

Snow! What I wouldn't give for some coolness, she thought, as her eyes trailed enviously after a young woman dressed in an ornately decorated yet simple abaya robe.

"I bet that feels just like wearing a nightdress, cool and comfortable. I wish I had the confidence to wear something like that."

"The abaya is not about confidence. It is about traditional. As you say, it is practical—it is cool and protects from the sun because so little skin is exposed. And it has the added benefit of providing protection from the unwanted advances of men."

"I always took you for a boobs and bum sort of man," she threw at him.

"You are right. But you are also wrong. I love, as you do, curves. You love it in your architecture, and I love it in my women."

"Women *plural*," she said. "How convenient that your rules allow men to have multiple wives but a woman can be murdered for just one transgression.

"I did not make these rules, and I do not abide by them. I appreciate beauty. In nature. In art. In women. Just because I am a connoisseur of many things does not make me a collector. In affairs of the heart, I am monogamous."

His eyes narrowed as he stared at her. She caught the fierce conviction in his eyes and she realised there were layers to him that she hadn't even fathomed, just as there were layers to her. Dark layers.

"I will show you to the guesthouse. You will find the air-conditioned rooms much cooler."

Tariq's stern good looks had always intimidated her as much as they'd enticed her. He stood over her, almost close enough to reach up and kiss his formidable lips. His tailored Western suit barely concealed the muscled body, she remembered too well and still thought about too much. It wasn't his cousin who was the Sultan of Seduction. It was Tariq—the Titan of Temptation.

As the driver continued to steer the golf buggy through the vast royal estate Melanie and Tariq sat in silence. Clearly, Tariq intended to ignore the sexual frisson that hummed between them, she thought as he sat rigidly beside her.

Why did his dismissal of her still hurt? Why was she allowing his cruel betrayal to still haunt her? Why couldn't she be an adult about her feelings? Surely she could relish the freedom of acting on her simmering desire. Couldn't she give herself the gift of one final fling? It didn't have to mean anything, did it? What if she bedded Tariq one more time to confirm she was truly free of him? Maybe taunt him with memories of what he was shunning? To teach him, once and forever, that she truly didn't care. It seemed like a good idea.

"We are here," he said, looking through her as the buggy drew to stop outside a large guesthouse. Made from the same rose-gold colour earth, the villa emerged naturally from the landscape. Surrounded by tall grass mastic trees underplanted with thyme and woody plants it was reminiscent of something she'd expect to find in the Sahara.

"Wow. In the blink of an eye I feel like I'm transported to Africa," she said.

For a fleeting moment she imagined a scene from the

movie *Out of Africa*, only Tariq was the lover born of the aristocracy, not her. And rather than be instantly enamoured with a commoner, his cold indifferent stare confirmed he was in no mood to enter the pages of a historic love story.

It was almost as though he was deliberately keeping his heart barren, and closed to her. The stark contrast to the intimacy they'd once shared triggered her anxiety and feelings of unworthiness.

She was a fool. A fool to dream of love. A fool to dream of one last night of passion.

She opened the door to the guesthouse and stepped inside without looking back. She closed the door firmly and pressed her back against the inlaid wood, relishing the coolness of the air-conditioned room.

Her heart still blazed from the last time he'd brushed her off and tonight had only inflamed the hurtful embers. He had erected an impenetrable fortress barring her from a legitimate life together and it was time to face facts.

One of them had to make the first move.

CHAPTER SIXTEEN

"One more thing," Tariq said, forcing the door as she remained with her back pressing it shut.

"You said you could give Salim the one thing I could not," he gritted. "*Love.*"

Her strange silence threw him temporarily.

He cleared his throat, clenching his hand around the door-knob. "Very well. Maintain your silence. But while you are here you will assume the role of the boy's primary caregiver."

He thrust his hand in the air as Melanie began to protest.

"You are to give Salim your devoted attention, the devoted attention a good mother would."

"I can't just abandon my architectural practice." She hesitated as though weighing her words. "I will care for Salim, of course. I will visit with him and sit with him as often as my work allows."

"You will not work. You will not need to. Money will no longer be your concern."

"Are you kidding me? Do you have any idea of the sacrifices I've made to get where I am in my career? No one, no man, no self-opinionated Sheikh, will tell me what to do.

Never." Her face flamed with raw and, dare he admits it, regal passion.

It was as though disobedience had been bred into every cell of her body he thought as she refused to submit. It was as tantalising as it was testing. For an uncontrollable moment, he wondered what it would be like to take to her to his bed. To take a woman not made frigid with blinding loyalty to the Crown. To take a Western woman not rendered lifeless with her submissiveness. To take a woman he knew enjoyed the pleasures of sex.

A woman who felt herself his equal, not his inferior.

He frowned as the common sense born of duty returned. Melanie was strong, talented, clear-sighted—the very qualities that made her so attractive. But she would never be a good, dutiful, obedient Avana woman. She would, and rightly so, insist on making good use of her intelligence. Was it wrong to expect her to sacrifice her career to mother a child who was not even hers?

He regarded her thoughtfully. "Your masculine energy is very strong," he said. "You have the spirit of a warrior, I admire that, but you do not balance it with that of a woman. Why is that?"

What is she resisting he wondered? What is she afraid of?

She blanched. Her bewilderingly beautiful brows knitted in a frown as though fighting his compliment with the same energy she summoned to rebuke his criticism.

"What does my energy have to do with anything?" she fired at him. "And who said a woman had to be balanced? I've never heard of anything more sexist and demeaning, and completely prehistoric." She stared at him with the same intense scrutiny as his hawk. The same fierce determination. The same watchful, furious gaze.

And to his consternation he felt something precariously

like enjoyment. As a child he had enjoyed table tennis, it struck him with a mix of childish delight that she would make a formidable opponent. On the table and in bed. All they needed was a couple of balls, a paddle, and some stamina.

He indulged his fantasy momentarily. Ping Pong was a game of skill. It took patience to win. Ping Pong was like a fine, well-aged concubine—it took years to learn her tricks.

We are not engaging in sufficient foreplay, he thought, enjoying the prospect, knowing how much more beautiful her eyes became when they were fuelled with formidable fire.

"There you go again, diluting your power with your defensiveness. What you are you afraid of?" he lobbied provocatively. "It's as though, on the one hand, you want to love the child, and on the other you are terrified," he said, realising as he spoke the words, that this was his truth.

She was terrified of caring too much just as fear caused his chest to quake. Or was he projecting onto Melanie his own anxieties? His fear of loving and risking the devastating pain he knew from experience love exacted?

His gaze rested on the bed, commanding a supreme position in the room. He must not cede the game prematurely.

"You will obey, and you will be pleased you did," he rallied, hitting her with the force of his command, hoping his words proved prophetic. Either way, he would be spared the pain of caring for the boy. He would be spared the guilt that Salim would not know a mother's love. He would be spared the fear that the closer he got the deeper the pain would thrust should anything happen to either of them.

"You have been in the West too long. You have learned to devalue and disrespect the role of a mother," he said, advancing his stance with a sidespin. "Your culture has been successful in its manipulation that only a working woman has power. In my culture, there is no greater role than being a mother. We do not measure a mother's worth by how much money she earns, by her salary, her title, or any of those other things your culture manipulates you to value," he said, employing a variety of shots to weaken her resolve. "Your worth is not determined by your economic success, but by your contribution to a better world. Being a mother achieves that in spades."

"No one has manipulated me. I have made my own choices, my own decisions," Melanie said. "I am striving to add to a better world—architecture, great architecture, achieves this. And I have followed the path that gives me the greatest joy."

She chopped her hands through the air, as though she was hacking through her own lies.

"Perhaps," he said, dubiously. "But as you speak your truth can you not hear for yourself the tremble, the quiver, the ache that suggests that your words do not ring true."

"No, Tariq, I can't," she said, throwing her arms, defensively across her chest.

"How will you know you would not enjoy the role of mother? How do you know you will not find fulfilment? How can you be sure that this thing you do, this architecture—" he said, dismissively, splaying his hands as he spun around and swept them toward the palace, "how can you really know that a raising a child will not bring you greater joy?"

Hadn't his own mother never given herself the time, never learned the patience, never initiated regular play, love, and contact with him as a boy? Leaving him instead to be raised by a succession of schoolmistresses and masters. No better than being a foster child—an orphan. Tariq's thoughts spun to Salim. No, he would not allow that same fate to befall his brother's child.

"Salim's mother is dead," he said, "but you will assume

this role and you will devote yourself wholeheartedly," he raised his voice, deliberately "He will never know what I grew up believing—that a job was more important to my mother than time spent with her son."

His words shook him, as much as they shook her. The colour drained from her face. A noticeable quiver to her lips and quickening of her breath announced she was ready to submit.

It wasn't the foreplay he had intended. It wasn't what his manual of seduction instructed. It wasn't what he knew would make it easy to claim her. To do this they should talk to each other softly, trading compliments on the beauty and crispness of their shots. Instead he had self-destructed.

"Mother's Day is not one day a year but should be, and will be every day. And your job as Salim's mother will start today."

CHAPTER SEVENTEEN

How could she have let herself imagine, even for a moment, that there would be anything between them? She had fooled herself into thinking that she had come here to tell Tariq about Salim. She had tricked herself into trusting that magically he would promise her the two-parent happily-ever-after-family fantasy she had deluded herself into believing.

She hadn't accomplished a single intention—let alone take the ultimate risk and gone for her dream. Worse, she had seriously under-estimated his cruel coolness and obsessive need to be in control.

She'd been naive in her assumption that her life would go on, that she could immerse herself in her work, and run her architectural practice at a distance. She had deluded herself into thinking that somehow the mothering genes she felt had evaded her would miraculously manifest and fulfil her need to prove herself worthy.

It wasn't that she didn't want to succeed, but because she didn't know how to be a mother. Her own mother was hardly a role model. She had never shown her any love. All she'd ever done was rant to her father how having children was a distraction; complain endlessly about how having children had derailed her career; whinge incessantly that her own daughter had stolen her limelight.

Melanie placed her hands over her ears, trying to silence the violent rages, the wild words, the terrifying tirades which hammered through her shoulders, her throat, her chest, with the same intensity she had felt as a child as her mother's venomous words had assaulted her. She told herself, convinced herself, that it was a relief when her mother ignored her and then finally abandoned her for good.

Everyone had told Melanie how much she looked like her mother. Which is why she'd dyed her naturally long Nordic-blonde hair black and abandoned the feminine look and attire her mother favoured and which was so flattering. And it was why she had assumed, that just like her mother she didn't have a maternal bone in her body.

She would make a shit mother. Which is why she now found the prospect of domestication so threatening. Her biggest fear was inflicting the same searing hurt on her son as her mother had on her own daughter.

Wasn't that the reason Melanie had given her son to her sister? Charlie was born to be a mother. She'd always been maternal. While Melanie was happily playing with building blocks and toy cranes and creating houses and communities and simulating life on her Sim's series of video games, her younger sister was obsessed with her dolls and acting out happy families.

In a cruel twist of horrible fate, Charlie's ovaries had denied her the one role in life that would make her truly happy. Wasn't that the reason Melanie had kept Salim a secret? She knew Tariq was a man of tradition—it was why he had rejected her in the first place. Melanie had always sensed he'd demand his child be raised in Avana with him.

Without her.

Her chest filled with anger and hurt. Her mind forcibly rejected that reality. Salim deserved to be raised by someone who cared about him, not a straight-jacket of centuries-old superstitions and customs.

Maybe she shouldn't tell Tariq. She would wait until Salim was well enough to return to America and she had found another architecture commission to be certain she would be able to provide for him and then she would leave.

And then she would never see Tariq again.

The only problem was she felt wracked with guilt and shame. What woman could give up her child, regardless of how motivated she was or how much she attempted to reconcile the abandonment of a child with an altruistic motive?

A shit mother.

What sort of mother would make it a condition of the adoption that her child must never know the truth?

A shit mother.

What sort of mother would never ever allow any photos to be sent to her or uploaded to social media?

A shit mother.

What sort of mother never made contact once she left?

A shit mother.

Her mother had walked out the door and never looked back. Literally. Instead, she had become completely, narcissistically obsessed with herself.

And now her daughter was doing the exact same thing.

It was true, rotten dates didn't fall far from the palm tree.

The only thing saving Melanie from feeling truly worthless was that she was good at architecture. Not just good—she was gifted.

Architecture blocked her shame and guilt. The only way to keep the demons at bay was to stay busy. *Insanely busy,* And pour her heart and soul into something that gave her purpose.

Now Tariq had the nerve to say she didn't have to work. Well, she thought, wrenching open the small night bag with the clothes she'd hastily thrown together, Tariq's command was less of a 'she didn't have to work' and more of a royal decree.

She strode to the far end of the room and hurled a sturdy pair of black ankle boots into the colossal walk-in wardrobe. Tariq had made it perfectly clear that while she was under his roof she was to assume the role of primary caregiver.

Did he have any idea what he was asking? Did he have any idea why she struggled to yield? Did he have any idea of the unpalatable truth? Her peers would never view parenting as a gold star on her professional resume.

Of course not. If he did, rather than welcome her with open arms, he'd banish her from their lives. Melanie raked her fingers through her hair.

What a bloody mess.

CHAPTER EIGHTEEN

"Those bloody mongrels!" Tariq's voice roared across the courtyard. Startled, Melanie looked up from her drawing board. He was carrying a sedated lion in his arms. His face was taut with rage and strain, and something else? Tears? Were those tears in his eyes, she wondered as he lowered his gaze?

"What has happened?" she said running to his side.

"Albanians," he spat. "The treacherous animals. We had already negotiated the lions' release, but no, they reneged on their agreement. They held their lying, greedy, corrupt hands out for more money. Look at the poor thing." Tariq cradled the lion in his arms. Its skin draped in saggy folds over ribs which threatened to poke through his matted fur.

Melanie didn't need degrees in veterinary nursing to see how malnourished the animal was as it lay limp in Tariq's arms, a shell of its former magnificent self. "What can I do?"

"They need proper hospital care," he said, gesturing to a pair of lions being unloaded from their purpose-built crates. "Follow me to the hospital I will need you to feed Bassam."

"Me?" she squeaked. It seemed the fates had decided that

she was going to be marinated in motherhood, Melanie thought wryly. First to an injured lion and then her own wounded child she mused looking at her fierce desert warrior king as he strode ahead.

She glanced towards the fountain of lions, as she hurried after Tariq. Somehow she would summon the spirit of a lioness and protect Tariq's baby cub, she vowed. And somehow she would learn how to be a mother to his son.

She listened as she watched him caring for the wounded animal.

"They stay in these inhumane cages built during the Cold War of the 1970s, walk and sleep on cement floors, and suffer anxiety and get nervous from having people stare at them all day. Then to top it off their owners just walk away leaving them to die in their cages. It's heartbreaking," Tariq said, lifting a giant paw as the vet nurse joined them and inserted a saline drip.

She discovered that the pride of lions had been removed as planned and paid for by Tariq from a private zoo ravaged by civil war. But bureaucratic delays acerbated by corruption meant that Tariq had been unable to take them to their new home. 11 animals in total had been seized in an international clampdown on animal cruelty.

"Fortunately we got them before their physical health deteriorated irreversibly, but they've suffered psychologically," Tariq said.

It didn't escape Melanie that their saviour was also damaged psychologically by people who should have cared for him.

"So you kidnapped them?"

"No, I rescued them," Tariq growled.

"Isn't that against the law?" It wasn't that Melanie thought Tariq had behaved wrongly, far from it. All anyone had to do was look at the poor lion. She knew that, like Tariq, any physical scars would mend but internal wounds were harder to heal. The people who treated the lions so cruelly had no more right to own these creatures than—

She bit her lip trying to silence the truth that coiled around the hospital bed. But she couldn't deny the facts. They had had no more right to own these defenceless creatures than she had any right to claim her son.

A sudden chill pulsed down her neck and into her chest. When Tariq discovered the truth of Salim's parentage would he act as swiftly, and seize his son as his rightful possession? Would he argue he was rescuing Salim from his unfit mother she wondered, fearfully aware of how readily people legitimised their actions.

"I don't believe anyone should keep any living being in captivity," Tariq gritted, wrapping a bandage around the lion's massive paw. "The owner is deluded if he thinks he can intimidate me with lawsuits," he clenched his fingers around the opposing edges of the bandage and pulled tight.

And as for the Albanian government, they had repeatedly postponed the lions' departure. Lives were at stake. Animals are living beings just like us, they have the right to live in freedom. I help these animals because, contrary to what you may believe, I'm a normal human."

Human, yes. Normal, no. Sheikh Tariq na Hassir was the most powerful man on planet earth.

"I cannot and will not stand impotently and see these animals suffer. It is intolerable to allow them to die of hunger without doing anything, waiting for the legal right to do what is morally correct. This is our duty as human beings. Politicians and law-makers often forget that."

His passionate conviction made her respect but also fear him. Now that Tariq had the lions secured under his protection nobody would be able to claim them. And now he had for all intents and purposes claimed Salim, other than divine intervention, nothing and nobody would be able to claim their son either. Certainly, not her.

The longer she stayed, the closer Tariq would get to discovering the truth. She would have no diplomatic protection, her Government had no jurisdiction in Avana. Her only chance was to flee the country or face the consequences of Tariq's ability to undermine other nations' processes of justice—no matter how flawed.

She would be wrong to underestimate him, just as they would be wrong to disrespect the innate disposition of the king of the jungle when it awoke from its slumber. Lion's don't become doves. Lies don't become truths.

CHAPTER NINETEEN

The next day she'd soaked up all the humidity, exploring Tariq's estate while he skilfully evaded her, God knows where. But today, she thought, she was glad of the distraction. Last night she had seen a side of Tariq which both excited and frightened her. She had tossed and turned all night. She had awoken to a note pushed under her door telling her that he had assigned one of his personal assistants to help her explore.

“Despite Avana's rich history, when Tariq arrived back from his overseas education on the island, it was nothing more than a desolate slab of desert,” Matt Schama, the adventure guide Tariq had assigned to Melanie, told her.

"There was just the sand and the hills; there were no trees or animals," he said. “Before the arid, barren island could be transformed into the refuge for wildlife that it is today, an astounding three million trees had to be planted. Tariq wanted to make Avana very lush from the start; it was part of his greening of the desert program—the same principle that was applied to Abu Dhabi and Dubai,” Matt explained.

Melanie loved learning more about the area and she began

to fall in love with the complex, fascinating country and the resilience of the people.

“Despite the odds and the fact that Avana is surrounded by ocean and its soil has an unusually high level of salinity, various tree species now thrive. Several different trees, both local varieties, and some brought over from Africa were planted. The animals followed."

There was that Out of Africa theme again, Melanie noted. Wondering what spell it wove over Tariq.

"Initially Tariq wanted the island to be a sanctuary for endangered Arabian wildlife, and the Arabian oryx was his focus," continued Matt.

“Unfortunately, the oryx—a white antelope with a distinct shoulder hump and long straight horns —had lived a cursed life. In the early 1980s, over-zealous hunters decimated the natural population of the handsome creatures. They were occasionally killed for their meat, but it was mainly their horns that attracted hunters to them; their horns were kept as trophies," Matt said.

“Dedicated to reviving the world’s population of Arabian oryx, Tariq tracked down captive oryx at a zoo in Phoenix, Arizona, which has a similar climate to Avana’s desert plains,” Matt continued.

"His determination is unrivalled,” Melanie said, voicing her thoughts.

"Yes, what His Highness wants, His Majesty gets."

That was what she was afraid of, she thought miserably.

"A few oryx were brought to the island from Phoenix for breeding and we now have over 500 here," Matt added. "Remarkably, thanks to captive breeding programs in Avana and around the globe, the Arabian oryx was declared no longer extinct in the wild.”

‘Wow! That’s amazing,” Melanie said, with uncharacteristic gusto. Had she seriously underestimated Tariq's character? A feeling of pride washed over her as she studied the diverse group collection of animals. His willingness to help those most at risk was a trait she admired. She only wished he wanted to fight for her too. Why couldn't he want her? She was endangered too.

"More than another 1000 have been born here and released," Matt said. "Some have been given to Jordan and some have been released into the desert region near the palace. As for how they're fending for themselves in their new home, the oryx's only predators are humans, so they now rule the roost. Everyone keeps their distance."

Melanie thought to herself how much she shared Tariq's despair and cynicism at how predatory humans are to their own kind and how she now better understood why Tariq had walled himself off.

She should do. She had too. Walling herself off with architecture all these years so she wouldn't have time to think about him and the love they had once shared. And he had walled himself off by only loving animals incapable of abandoning him.

"The cheetahs won't go anywhere near them because of their horns," Matt said, "They end up chasing the cheetahs," he laughed.

Melanie laughed uncomfortably as she thought about the invisible horns Tariq seemed to wield anytime she came near.

"The group of cheetahs and 20 or so giraffes that inhabit Avana definitely raise eyebrows. And a few questions. The Sheikh's time spent in eastern and southern Africa in his early 20s can account for the abundance of exotic animals that now reside on the island—after all, what do you buy a sheikh who has everything? A tower of giraffes, of course," Matt laughed.

"So that was where his fascination for Africa began. How on earth did they all arrive?" Melanie asked.

"Some came to the island by boat or plane, but many of them were given to the Sheikh as gifts, by people who either admired his cause—or wanted to cultivate his favour," explained Matt.

I'd like to cultivate Tariq's favour, she thought, the only problem was she didn't know how.

"Tariq decided he wanted to do something to bring more kindness into the world—to show that there are people who care about animals and doing something to protect those most vulnerable. He wanted to dispel the myth that all sheikhs do is buy gold cars and spend a filthy amount of money on themselves. Tariq's not like that."

Yes, she was discovering that fast. She should have been thrilled. But she wasn't. It only made it harder not to love him. "So he decided to share his vision with the world and open up the island of Avana to the public?" Melanie said, noticing with concern the way her voice trembled as she spoke. She didn't understand why, but hearing about Tariq's magnificent kindness sent crazy rivulets of joy, fast-moving electric currents of energy, racing through her.

"Yes—he doesn't usually let people into his sanctuary. You're the first. You must be very special to him."

Special?

Tariq hadn't given any indication that he thought she was in the least bit special, but the mere suggestion caused her heart to beat erratically.

"Conservation remains a priority for all on the island, and the wildlife have continued to flourish over the years," Matt said, unaware of the tumultuous feelings his disclosure ignited every time she heard of Tariq's activism.

"Avana is now home to hundreds of species of native and

exotic wildlife, many of which are critically endangered. They range from small Ethiopian hedgehogs to soaring reticulated giraffes; a few predators, including a pack of hyenas, and hundreds of migratory birds that nest on the island throughout the year. The island's captive breeding program releases a number of animals to roam free in the wild again, giving vulnerable species a chance to rebound in their natural habitat."

Melanie's thoughts drifted to their son. By wanting to prise Salim away from his ancestral environment was she hindering his ability to rebound from the accident? Was she selfishly depriving Salim of his natural habitat, his culture, his people—his birthright?

Was she going to make a terrible mistake?

CHAPTER TWENTY

How hard could it be? She wondered, stepping inside the hospital room Tariq had installed. She'd Googled how to be a mother. The results were promising. She didn't have to be a perfect mother, she quickly discovered as the first result displayed on her iPhone. She could be a good mother, otherwise known as a Good Enough Mom.

According to the article, as long as Melanie did her best to teach Salim how to live life to the fullest; Be there for him when he needed her; Teach him the importance of self-worth; Provide food, shelter, and love; Be a good example to him; Make time to have fun with him, she could qualify for 'good enough.'

The added complication that her son was still in a coma gave her the opportunity to practice, she assured herself, nodding her thanks as the nurse left to give her privacy.

"Hello Salim," she said, quietly. She stood by his paediatric bed, conscious she was standing as stiff as one of Tariq's security men. A knot gritted in her throat as she looked at the maze of tubes helping him to breathe. He looked so peaceful, so calm, so beautiful. She threaded her fingers together as they began to twitch. What's wrong with you, she asked, silently.

"He won't break," the nurse watching over Salim said softly.

"Can he hear me?" Melanie asked.

"No one knows for sure," the nurse said. "I pray to Allah, I never know if he really hears me, but I feel better."

Did Melanie deserve to feel better? How long was she going to punish herself? Tentatively she stretched a finger toward her sleeping son. She slipped her finger under his tiny palm.

A hot stream of what she could only describe as love shot through her, flooding her heart. She felt her eyes sting. Not with sadness but with indescribable happiness, She hadn't realised how much she had been missing. The only thing that had dulled her loss during all the years they were parted was work. Hard work. She worked harder than ever during those years and now she realised any happiness she had felt had been fake. This was real. This was authentic. This was true.

Melanie opened the book she had found on one of Tariq's extensive bookshelves. Lined with thousands of ancient manuscripts, the discovery of the children's book had surprised her. *The Prince* had also been one of her favourites as a child.

She fingered the pages, inhaling the sweet scent of ink and paper. As she did so she remembered fondly the evenings her father would spend reading to her as she lay in her bed wide-eyed and not in the least way inclined for sleep. But the story encouraged her to dream and it was not long before she closed her eyes and yielded to the alchemy of magical realms she one day hoped to dwell and her architecture inspired her to reach.

When fans and critics of her work called her buildings out of this world she smiled inwardly. They would never know a child's book lay behind her inspiration.

She sat in the soft camel-skin chair someone had thoughtfully placed beside Salim's bed. Then changed her mind and decided to stand. It all felt too formal. Too distant. Too detached. She stood beside Salim and leaned over, just as her father had. Only this time, unlike her father who had kissed her asleep, as she placed, a kiss upon his cheek she prayed inwardly that he would wake.

A sob rose in Melanie's throat. She lifted her face and looked at her son, who lay still, hands folded like a mourning angel. She lowered her face to his again, and let her lips settle on his skin, feeling the warmth and life that still pulsed through him. But still he didn't wake.

She was suddenly struck by his beauty and innocence. She was suddenly aware of his fragility and his vulnerability. The awareness that within her reach lay a child uninfected by the world. He had been raised by two loving people. Her sister, and Tariq's brother, Zayed. They loved him unconditionally. They wanted him. They had not raised him like her mother had reared her—to believe he was a nuisance, a mistake, a regrettable error. Nor did they subscribe to the belief that he was conceived in sin—tainted from birth.

Charlie and Zayed had told Melanie to always remember that Salim was born from love, that one day she would understand the real purpose behind his conception. Melanie had thought they both spoke in riddles. That they were being kind. They were trying to assuage her guilt. But no matter what they said she always felt like the dirty girl.

'*Let it go, Mel.*'

Melanie's heart stopped. She turned and looked around, knowing her sister wasn't there. But she had heard her sister's voice in her head, as clear as though she was next to her. Not a request this time, but an order. And with it came the recognition that Melanie had punished herself for too long. It wasn't enough that her own mother had made her feel like shit, but that she'd allowed herself to be victimised by her.

No matter how many affirmations she had done, no matter how many therapists she had gone to, no matter how hard she worked, she had persecuted herself. She had harboured and fed the toxic belief for three gruelling years that she was worthless. Like a virus, the cancerous thought had spread toward all her relationships, especially the ones that mattered most. Tariq and Salim. Causing her to keep them at a distance. Infecting her life with crippling pain.

'Why can't you settle for less?'

Melanie snorted. Don't listen to mom. Think like a queen. A queen wouldn't think crappy thoughts about herself, Melanie affirmed. Nor would the mother of the rightful heir to the kingdom of Avana. Nor would the mother of a prince tolerate any criticism of her son. Not just any son, but the son of a king. A sheikh. A formidable yet much-loved ruler. Everybody was flawed, she affirmed, glancing at the small scar above Salim's eyebrow. The issue is how much we chose to dwell on the negative.

'You're worthless, I wish you'd never been born, you ruined my life.'

'Don't listen to Mom,' her sister urged. 'She'll fog your mind and turn your fears against you.'

'You think you're better than everyone else.'

Why not. What's the harm in loving myself first? Melanie thought.

"Once upon a time there was a beautiful princess," Melanie's voice rose above the growing din of her mother's taunts.

"And she was just like everyone else. She was worthy of love," she said, rewriting the story of her life as she began narrating the book that she hoped would change not just her life, but all their lives.

Melanie looked up from the pages of the book, as the nurse left the room. "It's okay to be scared, Salim," Melanie said to her son. Her voice softened, a mother's comforting murmur. "I'm scared too. This is all foreign to me. It's all new. But we'll get through it. And when you wake up, I promise I'm going to make it up to you. I'm going to make up for all the years we've missed."

'You're a useless mother.'

Melanie spun around. "No, mom, I'm not. Now go away. Don't talk to me again. You know, as in *Bambi*, 'if you ain't got nothing nice to say, don't say nothing at all."

A sudden movement startled her. The air rippled with the sweep of her hand as she pointed a finger toward the intruder. "Tariq!" A whoosh of air shot from her lungs. "How long have you been standing there?"

CHAPTER TWENTY-ONE

"Not long," he said.

"I was just leaving."

"There's no need."

"Yes," she stammered, her voice barely audible. "There is."

He watched as she hurried from the room, and then walked to the bed and lay the soft, pink, giraffe he had purchased in Paris beneath the three-year-old's arm. *Pink,* he affirmed Not blue—or brown or anything even moderately manly or remotely true to the animal's natural colours.

Melanie had been right. Tariq was so shut down, so closed, so hard-hearted he was incapable of showing emotion. His own upbringing had been so frozen of femininity, so malnourished in favour of warrior-like masculinity, so deliberate in the demarcation and devaluing of the female gender that as a result, he went about his life with no more emotion than a terracotta warrior.

A tide of anger surged through his gut and churned with the pain of his lost childhood. He clenched his fists. He wanted none of that for his brother's son, he realised with punching clarity.

He leaned over and stroked the child's hair. Tariq's heart kicked as Salim's eyes fluttered. Was it possible that, against all medical wisdom, the boy was aware of his presence?

Impossible. He was lost to everyone, deep in a coma from which the doctors said he may never wake. The irony, the injustice, the torture, Tariq thought, tightening his grip on the metal frame of the paediatric bed. He was powerless.

What did the child dream of, he wondered, as he watched the boy lying lost in his unconscious mind? Tariq envied the peacefulness that enveloped him. He was thankful the child knew nothing of the car crash that had killed his parents. At least he had been spared that unspeakable trauma.

Tariq's gaze drifted to the pink giraffe. It was the perfect totem to accompany Salim on his sleepy journey. Wide-eyed, the giraffe appeared to agree. Tariq remembered the words of the African shaman he had met on one of his many rescue missions to liberate endangered species. The gentle creatures, with their gracefully long necks, were believed to stretch into heaven. 'They are a spirit animal who wanted you to hold your head high and rise above trivial earthly desires', she had said.

'They have the ability to reach opportunities that are not available to others,' she had told him. 'It is also said that they can see the cosmic plans of the gods and inherently the possible future. As a spirit guide, the giraffe provides you the confidence to get through the toughest situations. Their luck will rub off on you as you come across great opportunities. You have to realise that these opportunities don't come around often so you have to grab them while you can.'

Longing flooded his body as he gazed at the child. More than anything he wanted to clutch the boy and cleave him to his heart and kiss him awake. It wasn't trivial to want the boy to rouse; it wasn't trivial to want the boy to gain consciousness. it wasn't trivial to want the boy to live.

His grandfather's words floated through the air. *Teach your children to love.* The very words Hamza had spoken to his own son, Tariq's father, only to find the wisdom fall on blocked ears. Wasn't this why there was so much hate in the world? People had stopped listening to their hearts.

Tariq's mind drifted to a news article he had read recently. A 10-year-old child whose family had escaped persecution for their beliefs under the hateful Taliban regime, hoping to find a safe haven from Islamic State terrorists in New Zealand, had been taunted and bullied at school. Feeling so much pain he had tried to commit suicide. The hate-riddled school children, the article said, had held a knife to his throat as they yelled, *Isis lover.*

Rage ripped through his chest. Melanie was right. The child needed love. All children needed love. The world needed love. What right did he have to deprive anyone of that?

Tariq clutched his heart, feeling the pain, the emotions, the trauma he had suppressed for so long, flood to the surface. No, he vowed, clenching his fists, Salim would never know hatred, brutality, nor quiet contempt.

Tariq had vowed never to become his father and yet as Melanie had so bluntly reminded him, he had become a tyrant. He had spent a childhood marinated in trauma. He lifted his hands to the soft toy of Simba which had been rescued from the car-wreck and now lay ever watchful, at the foot of Salim's bed. He lifted his paw and in a moment of punching clarity, he vowed he would dedicate his life to ensuring the boy's life roared with love.

He propped the toy back into a protective stance, his paws

outstretched toward the child, his long, powerful body splayed toward Salim. Tariq reached over and gently, tenderly, softly pressed his lips to the child's cheek. He felt his eyes water and before he could control the flow of raw emotion a tear, shaped like a diamond, plopped upon Salim's lips. But, unlike a fairytale miracle, his sleeping beauty did not wake.

Tears fell like a floodgate he was unable to stop, as though a valve in his garden had wedged itself open. Tariq watched transfixed as a finger of light from the setting sun anointed the tear in a prism of light.

How could he reach the boy? How could he save him?

He ran his hand across his chin, then leaned down and opened the musical case which lay beneath the child's bed. What had the doctors said? Sometimes music had the power to heal.

CHAPTER TWENTY-TWO

"Look out!'

Melanie looked up into the sky to see a parachutist propelling toward her.

"What the—" she exclaimed, unable to finish her sentence as the edge of the parachute draped over her, sending her sprawling across the ground.

"Hi, I'm Latifa,' the parachutist said, freeing herself from her harness. She strode out of the parachute and walked toward her. Latifa held out her hand toward Melanie, "I'm the unruly princess."

Melanie studied her as she unzipped her flaming red jumpsuit. Dressed in sneakers, jeans and T-shirt emblazoned with the words 'defiant,' she didn't look the least like a princess.

"You could have killed me," Melanie said. Taking Latifa's hand, she reluctantly allowed her to pull to her feet. Princess or no princess she wasn't about to be left flailing on the ground.

"I'm so sorry. Are you okay? A sudden gust blew me off

course. But I've been meaning to bump into you," she said, softly.

"Well, you certainly managed to do that,'" Melanie said, her voice croaked, winded from the fall.

"You're the woman who's going to steal my brother's heart," Latifa said, her black eyes dancing with delight. 'I'm thrilled to meet you."

"I'm sorry?" The princess was talking in riddles. Until now, she didn't even know Latifa existed.

"I knew it the moment I saw you arrive. And do you know why I'm so certain?" Melanie had no clue, but she didn't need to wait long to be illuminated.

"Tariq's like me," she said, gesturing to the compound where her brother's most recent rescuees were assembled. "We don't trust humans. I'm guessing he hasn't told you that."

"He barely speaks to me,' Melanie said. "He never even told me he had a sister."

"Don't take it personally. He's a retard when it comes to talking about his feelings—or his family."

"I can relate to that," Melanie said, surprised by how strangely familiar Tariq's sister was and how easily she confided in the strange woman who fell from the sky.

"So what's your story?" Latifa asked with a refreshing directness.

Melanie hesitated. She had no idea where to begin, least of all what she should reveal. And the princess, endearing, as she seemed, was no more familiar than a stranger.

But for some reason, which she couldn't explain, something about this brazen defiant woman intrigued her. If she hadn't just met her she would have sworn that they had been friends forever.

"Why did Tariq never mention you?"

Latifa bit her lip and kicked the ground. "All families have their secrets," she said when at last she spoke.

"My mother did a runner when I was six-years-young. I don't trust people. I prefer buildings," Melanie said. The habit of privacy was too deeply ingrained for her to say more about her damaged childhood, but for some reason she wanted to confide in someone close to Tariq and she figured it was a good place to start. She knew for certain she didn't want to go near the topic of their own child.

Latifa smiled. "I appreciate your honesty. My brother's like a building. He's got good foundations. He's loyal, steadfast and true. But he needs remodelling. Our shitty upbringing was like a maelstrom of exploding bombs. A desert storm of destructive proportions. You know," she said, shrugging her shoulders, "the way that wars always destroy things that are beautiful.

"All that family drama was like adding a whole wing of hateful rooms to a beautiful structure, you know in all sorts of different styles, and all the influences that impacted him."

Latifa glanced toward the hospital wing, "Something tells me you'll be able to refashion him, bring out the best."

"What makes you so certain he wants to change?" Melanie said.

"Because you have something he wants. Something he needs. Something he doesn't even know he desires."

There she was talking in riddles again. But this time, instead of amusing her, it made Melanie feel uneasy. Uneasy in the way that a ticking clock made her feel.

"I don't usually do remodels. I prefer new builds. Starting from scratch without the complications of trying to remedy the wrongs of the past," she said, deliberately misunderstanding her.

"You have my permission to do a demolition job. Smash

through his wounded façade, free the soul inside," Latifa said, throwing her head back defiantly.

Melanie wanted to say, 'Tariq doesn't have a soul.' But she'd seen how he had been with the animals. How caring and kind. And she'd seen that cute, little pink giraffe he had hidden behind his back when he went to visit their son.

Despots are incapable of that sort of caring. Deep within, in a place she could trust, she knew Tariq held something redeemable. And she was intrigued whether his defiant sister could shed light on the man within and the wounds she couldn't see.

He kept everything close to his chest. Besides Melanie wasn't sure she wanted to take on such a massive project. But she did want to understand more about her child's father. His nuances, what made him tick, why he was the way that he was.

She'd always been curious. And wasn't she working on being less judgmental? What was she thinking, she quickly censored? She wasn't in the least bit interested in what made Tariq tick. What interested her more was how she and her son were going to escape the long-reach of his wrath when he discovered the truth.

"As fascinating and flawed as your brother is, I'm afraid I don't have the time, nor the inclination to take on a project of such magnitude," Melanie said.

Latifa scoured the infinite desert. "Do you think Tariq will let you leave?" she said. "If so you are naive. This goes deeper than what you want, about what I want, this is about putting right a wrong."

Melanie felt her gut churn.

"I don't get you."

"Salim,' Latifa said, simply.

"What about Salim?"

Latifa shrugged and climbed onto the Arabian mare a servant had brought to her. As she prepared to ride toward the palace she turned.

"Don't you think it strange that Salim has Tariq's eyes?"

CHAPTER TWENTY-THREE

"So, you met my sister? What did she have to say?" Tariq asked, tension etched on his face. He looked up into the sky as the hawk made wide sweeping circles above them, as though intently curious on the conversation going on below.

"Nothing much," Melanie said.

"Latifa never says nothing. If she were adept at silence my father—" he hesitated and studied his hands as his fist clenched into tight balls. "If Latifa were less rebellious she wouldn't have gotten into so much trouble. But I don't blame her for what happened. I blame my father. What he did was unforgivable."

"What about your father?" Melanie searched his face noticing the knotted lines that etched his brows. The way he stood, the rigidity of his body, told her that understanding the dynamic between his father's relationship with Tariq and his siblings held the key to knowing what made him so distant and cold.

"Latifa's story is hers to tell. But I can tell you that my father was a blow-thirsty, bitter, bastard," bitterness bled from his words, causing her stomach to flip. “He was a bastard to all my sisters. To all women in fact. Actually, he was a bastard to everyone.” His voice was low and hard., but he no longer cared how much he gave away. He wanted her to understand.

Melanie said nothing. Urging him on with her silence.

He hadn’t meant to blurt out his family drama. But she was so still, so silent, unlike other women. Unlike his wife who had talked incessantly and probed and probed, never stopping to listen, until in frustration he closed down completely.

But Melanie was different. With her big, wide, watchful eyes and her even huger heart, she was like a giraffe—quiet, caring, and watchful. Until under the intensity of her gaze, he felt compelled to fill the silent void.

He began hesitantly, unsure of her reaction. Would she think of him as others did? That he was just like his father. Which should suit him just fine. If they were smart, they would keep their distance. Only for some disturbing reason, what Melanie thought of him mattered.

“My father didn’t start out being a tyrant. He loved my mother with total abandon. She took advantage of that. She spent his money with the gushing velocity of the oil that springs from the bowels of Avana. But that was not what broke him. He had plenty of money. Too much money. Sometimes my family’s wealth disgusts me. Not all of it is honestly gained. But that is another story. My father's story.”

"No one begins this life planning to be a tyrant," Melanie offered. There is so much suffering, so much pain, so much trauma—" she began.

“Lies!" he interrupted. "What really broke him was her lies, her deception, her deceit. Had she not insisted on concealing the truth perhaps all would have been forgiven.”

Melanie shifted uncomfortably on her feet, as though the hot sand was burning through the soles of her sandals.

“He discovered too late the affair she’d been continuing behind his back—our backs," he added, with a force that surprised him, "under his very nose with his most trusted advisor. It's one thing to elope with a stranger. Another to flee with your husband’s esteemed confidant."

“Your mother must’ve had her reasons," Melanie offered, tentatively. "You said it yourself, he was a bastard. And I've heard from many others in the little time I have been here, of his corrupt and cruel propensities."

"It's true. But at least he was real,” Tariq said. “What you saw was what you got. He didn't lie to me. Life taught me a lesson I will never forget. Fear not the cruel person—be on guard for those who deceive you with kindness."

"It was a long time ago. You’re still angry," she said, reading his pain. Pain that he no longer denied, but could not bring himself to reveal more fully.

“No,” he said, tension knotting his throat. "I’m not angry. I'm grateful. My mother made me a realist, not an idealist. And my father…well, let’s just say dates don’t drop far from the tree.”

“That’s not who I see," Melanie said. "You’re nothing like your father."

And for the first time in many moons, he felt relieved. “Come on, there’s someone I want you to meet,” he said, taking her hand.

CHAPTER TWENTY-FOUR

"This is Johara," Tariq said, rubbing a powerful hand along the broad neck of a horse. "It's Arabian for jewel. This Arabian horse is one of the world's oldest breeds. Bred by the Bedouin and used as a desert warhorse throughout the ages, these precious and majestic animals have evolved in ways to withstand the desert's unrelenting environment."

The crystal clear waters and bright blue skies that encircled the kingdom of Avana provided a striking contrast to Johara's wispy white mane and alabaster coat. Everything felt magical, Melanie thought, as Tariq bent toward the horse's hooves and lifted his foot.

"Stronger-than-normal hooves help them navigate the rugged terrain, while thinner skin and higher tails keep them cool under a smouldering sun. In the 18th century the agile, good-natured breed was introduced to Europe and became a popular choice for royal families. In fact, it was an Arabian horse named Marengo that carried Napoléon Bonaparte to safety at the Battle of Marengo in 1800. Today the horse's distinct characteristics—and the strong bond they form with their keepers—makes the Arabian horse a breed that is treasured right around the globe."

What I wouldn't give to be kept by you, she thought, strangely envious of the languid, sensuous, strokes he swept across Johara's legs. "You make them feel safe," she said, realising as she spoke, that Tariq made her feel safe too. Rather than comfort her the feeling rankled. She didn't want to feel safe. Not here. Not with him. It was a mirage, and she was parched enough and thirsty enough for someone to want her to fool herself that her dream of a life with him, raising their son, was real.

Oblivious to her unease Tariq continued on, and she caught herself swept away by the passion and purpose he so clearly felt for animals that fell under his protection.

"We are fortunate," Tariq said, following her gaze, as it drifted toward the sea. "An abundance of marine and birdlife flock here, " he bent his gaze to her, magnetising her with his golden eyes. She felt like there was some mental disconnect happening between her brain and her loins. Here she was admiring wild beasts, and yet she didn't feel the least interested in feathers and fur and fish gills. But she didn't—couldn't—tell him that what really interested her was the softness of his skin, the coarseness of his hair, the hardness of his—"

Nope, she so couldn't go there.

"Endangered hawksbill and green turtles, pods of bottlenose dolphins and schools of black-tip reef sharks are often spotted within the island's marine conservation area," she said, opting instead to impress him with the knowledge she had gleaned from the day she had spent with Matt Turner. "It stretches out eight kilometres from the shore. A number of migratory birds flock to Avana and the neighbouring unspoiled Destiny Islands, making the pristine spot in the Persian Gulf a true nature lover's paradise."

God. She'd gone and said it.

Lovers.

Now what was going to happen, she wondered, as he studied her with primal appreciation.

Nothing. That's what happened.

No kiss. No fondle. Not even a grope.

Instead, Tariq began inviting her to dinner. His life was decidedly constrained, but over meals, they had enough privacy to talk at length about a wide range of subjects, including their childhood, something they had only just started discussing and had never touched on at University when they first met.

They found that they had led oddly parallel lives. They were both shy and reserved and had few trusted friends. They had been sent to a bewildering succession of schools. Tariq to seven and Melanie to five.

They had both emerged from their family experiences and disjointed schooling with a firm determination to be self-reliant.

They also expanded on what they had already discovered —that they both had difficult relationships with one of their parents. And that they had enjoyed special relationships with a grandparent. He with his grandfather and Melanie with her maternal grandmother. Tariq's relationship with his grandfather, however, was profoundly significant and had been cruelly broken under dramatic circumstances.

"I had gone with my grandfather to Jerusalem, and I was standing 10 feet away from King Abdullah, when my grandfather was assassinated by a Palestinian for his efforts to explore a political solution with Israel. I was 16 at the time,"

His breath caught and he stared sadly out toward the setting sun, and the blood orange sky. “I’m sorry. Even after all this time I still find it difficult to talk about it.”

“It must have been so traumatic. To witness that. To see that. Oh, Tariq. I’m so sorry.”

“We had gone to the mosque for Friday prayers. A gunman suddenly stepped out from behind a pillar and shot my grandfather in the head. I can still see his white turban roll to a stop in front of my feet. I can still see my grandfather’s entourage flee for their own safety, I can still see the gunmen turn, aim his pistol at my chest—and fire.”

Melanie gasped.

“Only the medal on the military uniform, a decoration that my grandfather had insisted I wear that morning, saved my life by deflecting the bullet. On that morning my brother and I became the crown princes and my father be**came** King. The rumours persisted that my grandfather had been assassinated on the orders of my father."

"Do you believe that?"

"What? That he ordered a hit on his own father. Sure. I wouldn't put it past him. He had a lot to gain. Recently it came to light it turns out he had a mental illness." Tariq shrugged. " I don't know what I believe. It seems like more convenient lies."

"To protect the Hassar reputation?"

"Diagnosis can't achieve that. Only actions can achieve that," he said.

"Then you have already succeeded," she said. "When he died his cruel legacy died too."

He shrugged, “Time heals they say. Only it doesn’t, not really,” he looked at her, his eyes pooling with strong emotion, drawing her within the velvet depths of his dark black eyes. "Some things, some feelings, some memories never die."

"That day fate spared you and now fate his spared Salim in a similar way. By all accounts, he should have died. But he was spared. There's a reason for that. A purpose, a destiny already written in the stars," she said.

Was now the time to tell him the truth. She wanted to. She really wanted to tell him that he had a son. That Salim was not his brother's child but his son and heir. But the timing still didn't feel right. He was retelling the story of the horrific murder, mourning, and reliving the savage murder of his beloved grandfather. She didn't want to add further shock.

The truth was he retold the story of the King's death in such vivid detail she could smell the terror, scent the blood, hear his anguished screams. No, now was most definitely not the time to tell him she had lied.

"Was it Islamic extremism that made your father so oppressive?" she asked.

CHAPTER TWENTY-FIVE

"For an educated woman you are very misinformed," Tariq said, his tone laced with sardonic derision.

He stood in front of her—a tall man, broad-shouldered and formidable, the starkly molded framework of his face highlighted by the spurt of flame from the torches.

He exuded authority and a compelling magnetism that still kept her pulse soaring. But Melanie's face heated under the sting of his criticism. She silenced her retort and looked steadily at him, imploring Tariq to enlighten her.

"Islam is not about oppression. It is not about murder. It is not about suppressing all that is beautiful. Beauty *is* God. God *is* love. Evil, malevolent men have taken the teachings of Mohammed and twisted them. Mohammed was just like Jesus. He was God's messenger on earth. Muslims believe as Christians believe, as many people believe, in the language of love."

"Which sounds like?" she tempted. She hadn't heard, nor seen, nor tasted anything that sounded in the least bit like the language of love and she was suddenly ravenous.

"God commands us to be of service to mankind. Service

to humanity. Service to ensuring peace and kindness and generosity. Above all we revere beauty. We honour and celebrate and dedicate ourselves to the beauty that Allah, the creator, God, call him what you like, has enabled us to create. This is the true path. It's what distinguishes us from animals."

Okay, so he wasn't taking the bait. It was probably just as well. She'd feast instead on the exhilaration of his powerful, politically astute mind. Intelligence was sex enjoying foreplay, she reconciled.

"Are you saying that rather than seek to dominate the world Islam encourages unity and equality among all individuals, regardless of age, colour, gender or social status? You don't support the creation of a totalitarian state?"

"Isis," Tariq said simply.

"Exactly," Melanie said, more confused than enlightened.

"Isis—capital I, little s, i, s— is not an organisation," he said, the force of his anger flaring in his eyes. "Isis was a woman. A goddess. An agent of healing. Those who took her name have taken this Truth and twisted her and made her an object of evil just like they did with the swastika in Indonesia. Just as they distorted Mary Magdalene, the Virgin Mary, and other powerful women.

Wow, could he be more sexier, she thought, intoxicated by his passion and wave of unexpected feminism.

"Sinister, flawed humans take strong powerful women and then turn the divine feminine into something malevolent. The world is in danger of being overcome by fear and tyranny. I for one stand against this. What does ISIS stand for?" he lobbied.

"Islamic State?" she ventured. It's what she'd heard time and again on the news, but as she spoke the words she realised the newsreaders and papers very rarely said this, instead they referred simply to ISIS.

"I and S—that is Islamic State. On there own they don't make sense. What organisation wants to be called IS? They should be called 'WAS'.... they are nothing," Rage ignited his words. "Rational, right minds know this."

Was he criticising her ignorance? Or trying to educate her to the truth. She decided on the latter and continued to feast on their foreplay. God, she could kiss him right now. He was so damned delicious. His face all flushed with impassioned conviction; His eyes ablaze with firm belief; His indomitable spirit enlarged by the rightness of his position.

"No, they not nothing," he corrected. "We must be on guard to the disease of apathy. They are evil. They seek to repress all that is beautiful. This is how you see their true face. They are the face of darkness. They make everyone wear black. They force women to cover and cower. They make everyone abandon the beauty of colour."

"You haven't done that. You're a champion of beauty," she said, suddenly understanding what drove him.

"Yes, we must recreate beauty. We must be the face of light. We must be the lamp of love." As he spoke the torch-light arched toward him, illuminating his amber eyes, sparking with intense emotion.

"The group's use of Islamic scripture is illegitimate and perverse. The practices employed by the Islamic State, who incidentally have no sovereign authority to speak on behave of Islam are explicitly forbidden by Islam—torture, slavery, forced conversions, the denial of rights for women and children, and the killing of innocents. It is abhorrent."

Melanie felt her respect and admiration for Tariq soar in the wake of the passionate conviction with which he spoke. She had misjudged him. She had been ignorant. And worse, she had been manipulated into believing all Islamic people supported the Islamic State.

"I will continue to lead my people to rise up against evil, to expose their distorted truths, to shed light on their lies, to fight against all that stands in the way of peace—their reign of terror will die. In the end, love wins. We know love wins." He looked at her deeply and intensely allowing the word to linger in the space that separated them.

"I'd like to believe that," she said. "Sometimes it just seems so—" she shrugged. "I don't know. It just seems like there is so much evil in the world. I just feel so powerless. But I'd like to do what I can. I'd like to help you create something beautiful here in Avana. Something to show the world that we care."

A smile danced across his lips. "You really are the most beautiful woman."

For a moment she was thrown with this unexpected compliment.

"You are beautiful not just on the outside but on the inside. Kindness, compassion, and open-mindedness. Beauty shines from your eyes and your heart," he said, drawing closer to her. "There is more that unites us than divides us, *habibti*."

She could hear her chest rise and fall as he stood in front of her, not taking his gaze from her face. She studied her toes, kicking the hot desert sand with her left foot.

Tariq lifted her chin with his long, tapered fingers so that her eyes met his. "Love wins," he said. He leaned toward her, and swept her chin in his palm, lifted her face to his, and pressed his sensuous lips to hers.

And kissed her.

CHAPTER TWENTY-SIX

The night pulsed with flickering candlelight as he raked his fingers through the soft curtains of her hair, the silkiness of her tresses flooded his palms, flowing over his hands. He laced his fingers around the back of her neck and pulled her to him, plundering her mouth with a raw, demanding kiss.

Their conversation had been erotic, arousing, enrapturing—igniting in his soul a passion he was powerless to pretend didn't exist. He wanted to play with fire. And he wanted to do it again and again until his mind was wiped of everything except his need for her.

He felt his soul merge with her as his lips touched her lips, his tongue tasted her tongue, and his breath breathed her breath until the pain of his past was extinguished.

He had been an obstinate, wilful fool to deny himself this pleasure. To deny her of this pleasure. Pride melted into her kiss. Ego dissolved into her mouth. Fear disappeared beneath her touch.

The quest to claim her driven not just by lust but by a

dangerous need to drive out the darkness that had gripped him for too long.

He claimed her mouth, again, and again greedily selfishly, hungrily, spurred by a passion to possess her that was both liberating and addictive. For once he wasn't thinking. Not analysing. Not controlling anything other than his desire to draw closer to her light.

He could feel the way her heart quivered. He could sense the way her pulse fluttered in her neck. He could taste the breathlessness of her desire. And he knew in this moment they were united.

He circled his hands around her waist and slid her into his lap. The glow of the firelight bathed Melanie's face in gold as if she'd been lit from within by molten amber.

"No, Tariq," she murmured, "I can't," her voice barely a whisper. But there was no denying he hadn't felt her desire as his hands ran over the silk of her dress. He cupped her breasts beneath the fabric, feeling the tiny torturous mound of her hardened nipples responding to his touch.

"Oh, God," she sighed, folding into him.

Everything felt inevitable as he cupped his hands beneath her bottom and lifted her in his arms. He was moving too fast, spiralling out of control but he no longer cared. United by desire, in this one act, they were at last together.

A sexual need so urgent and shocking engulfed him in a storm of desire so powerful that it extinguished every rational emotion, charging the chasm of need, filling the unrelenting void.

* * *

Shame covered her like a filthy, dark, oil slick. She wanted to dive into an oasis and scrub her past clean. She wanted to bury her guilt in the hot sand. She wanted to set fire to the secret that kept her imprisoned.

"I shouldn't have kissed you back," Melanie said, pulling her lips from his.

She wriggled in his arms until at last he set her on her feet. When her eyes met his all she could see was the burned heat and blaze of confusion. And all she could think of was his body, hard, and urgent against hers.

"I wanted to, God, I wanted to. I've been sitting there all night fantasising about it. But I can't. I mean, I did. But I shouldn't. What I mean is—" She found herself hoping desperately he would understand. The craving inside her had obliterated her fear of telling him the truth. If they were to have a future she needed to confess.

"Are you playing hard to get, *sheikha?"* His tone was raw, his voice thickened with emotion.

"Look there's no easy way to say it. There's something I haven't told you. Something you should know. Something—"

"Something I have already discovered."

"You have? And you're not mad?" She groped for the best way to respond.

"Mad? Why would I be?" His gaze shifted to her hands, and he lifted them to his lips. She felt a tiny shiver race through her. Her skin still burned from his touch. It was all so confusing.

"I thought—a relationship cannot lie in a bed of secrets."

"I never dreamed that it would be you. But now it seems so obvious."

"It does?"

"I am delighted." His eyes held hers. His tone was silky soft. "When can I see them?"

"Them?" her voice was shaky as she backed away.

"The drawings."

Melanie paced the width of the terrace and back again, so shocked she didn't know how to calm herself.

"I'm not angry," he said. "I know they'll be brilliant."

"I'm not following."

"It was Latifa's idea."

"Latfia?"

"That day you went out by yourself into the desert, she led me to you. I watched you. I saw what you were drawing. What you were designing. I saw that you were working."

Oh, god, he thought she wanted to confess to disobeying his decree that she didn't work. She desperately tried to compose herself. How could she tell him now? How would he react?

CHAPTER TWENTY-SEVEN

He had decided to pick a moment when she was her most relaxed, a time when she was most likely to trust him with those secrets she buried so deep within her soul. And now seemed like the perfect moment.

When his mouth was on hers, when his hands were holding her face and his tongue was buried deep into hers, it felt as though he could touch that part of her she kept walled off from him. It felt incredible and he wanted more. And wanting more meant he wanted it to mean something. For *them* to mean something.

The reckless heat of sexual frisson had subsided and in its place a warmth and intimate glow and a desire to connect more deeply rose. But rather than questioning her directly about her past, uncharacteristically he chose to probe gently, "Why did you become an architect?"

She looked thrown, which surprised him. But then she was used to his disinterest in her career.

"My dad encouraged me," she began, slowly. Her eyes trailed in the distance, and swept the night sky, as though she was erasing thoughts she dared not share.

“I remember he would always ask my opinion and ask me to design things for my bedroom when I was a toddler,” she said, her tone brightening. “So, it really started early and I knew that my father appreciated deeply my unusual talent. I’m grateful for that. I know many children aren’t so lucky.”

The unspoken trace of sadness he detected in her voice spoke to him. He understood too intimately, a child's insatiable need to have both parents love the child their union had created—regardless of their own hostilities. He understood what it felt like to try so hard to please others, that in the end you accepted failure and made a success of something you could control. Your career. Your hobbies. Your personal mission to make something good in the world.

“I wanted to make my dad proud," she continued. "I wanted to bring something beautiful into his life. My parent’s marriage was not a happy one. They would argue a lot," she tried not to look upset, but Tariq sensed the trauma of her childhood bubbling below her stoic surface.

“It was like living with a volcano. It was hard on my dad.”

Oh, yes, he could relate to that. Most definitely. Try living with a father with the disruptive, unpredictable, destructive energy of fifty volcanoes, he thought.

“And you?” he asked, gently, admiring her quiet strength, her steady determination. Admiring *her*. Just her. "How did you cope?”

She shrugged. “It was what it was. It was a lonely childhood. Architecture was my friend, my escape. To block out their arguments, I would retreat into my room and create fantasy worlds using paper, and cardboard, scissors and paste. So you know, sometimes good things can come from a chaotic personal life.”

Tariq felt his anger swell. Her childhood was not so

different from his own. Harsh, cruel, hateful. Perhaps, they were more similar than he realised, he thought, as appreciation grew. Rather than become bitter, she used and drew upon her childhood experiences to improve not just her life, but those impacted by her choices.

"I admire your positivity," he said, simply. He was aware that the words did not do his feelings justice. What he wanted to say was, 'I *love* your positivity. I love you," but such a statement came with a promise he was incapable of meeting. He had already let her down. He couldn't do it again. No matter, how deep his feelings were becoming.

"I'm not sure I'd call it positivity," she said, dismissing his compliment, "More of a survival strategy." She gave a feeble laugh and twisted her fingers over each other. "Reading about architects, and creating my own designs, was my escape from the conflict between my parents and my mother's unpredictable moods. Buildings were my friends."

The light caught the side of her cheek, illuminating the beautiful proportions of her face and Tariq thought to himself how utterly exquisite and gracious Melanie was. The vulnerability imbuing her words only made her more beautiful.

"My Dad always read to me at night before I went to sleep. He was obsessed by modern architecture and the role of geometry and new mathematics rather than notions of proportion and symmetry," Melanie said, oblivious to Tariq's conflicting thoughts.

"He introduced me to some of the greatest 20th-century champions of non-rectilinear organic forms—engineering pioneers such as Max Berg, Pier Luigi Nervi, Felix Candela, and Buckminister Fuller. They pushed new geometry and new materials, such as reinforced concrete, to their limit to create daring and beautiful structures. It didn't escape me, nor my father, that none of those pioneers were women."

"When we met you were studying mathematics—is the love you found in architecture as a child why?" Tariq asked.

"Yes, my dad inspired me. He introduced me to the language of science. I loved the way my father made numbers and physics, and fractals, and non-linear geometry exciting and thrilling. He gave me the ability to convey and create complex things in an incredibly simple way."

"Like Arabic art, " Tariq said.

"Yes, just like that," she smiled. "Architecture is my muse —I love her. My whole life is devoted to her. That's what I live on. I only wish sometimes she loved me back."

Her voice dropped into a deep sadness and made him want to do something to make her happy. He could not give her *his* love, but he could give her what she loved. He could give her the opportunity to relive her happy childhood and make her mark. He savoured the thought and allowed it to settle on his tongue as he continued to listen to her.

"When my dad finished reading to me I would close my eyes and think of those early pioneering architects and the problems they were trying to solve. They were so smart and audacious in their vision, they always figured everything out, as if they had magical powers. I wished that I had those same superpowers. I wished I knew how to make our house a happy place so my mother would come back to me and want to stay at home."

Her confession explained her behaviour, the way she kept him at a distance, why she struggled to accept help, the way she swatted away compliments. They all stemmed from her fear of being unworthy. She had been scarred by her childhood and then chosen a career in which men ruled.

Now he understood why she fought so hard to be

accepted, why her independence was so important to her. Nothing had come easily for her. She was a battler. She had to fight for everything—even the love and acceptance of the woman who should have loved her most.

Her mother.

CHAPTER TWENTY-EIGHT

"My mother went away a lot, and when she was there she wasn't there for me. I was a disappointment," she said, avoiding his gaze.

"So I got to spend a lot of time with my father. Growing up he instilled in me the belief that girls could do anything. Looking back now, I know that's easy to say when you're a man. Still, when I was five before my mother left, he started taking me to visit the best architecture in America. His favourite was Frank Lloyd Wright. Wright's buildings were beautiful but his designs still seemed too masculine to me, straight lines and towering peaks. Still, just seeing how Wright drew his inspiration from nature and approached architecture as a laboratory, experimenting with design concepts that contained the seeds of his architectural philosophy, inspired me."

"It is refreshing to meet someone who finds inspiration in the world around her," Tariq said.

Her gaze dropped to her lap as the compliment landed on her.

"It would be easy to succumb to the ugliness in the world.

I was lucky that my father fed my mind with such a healthy diet," she said. She looked up and met his gaze. Her cheeks flushed as though it felt wonderful to have his full attention.

"Then my dad took me to see the work of John Lautner. It was mind-blowing, Lautner had an apprenticeship in the mid-1930s with Wright but his work took off in an incredible direction. Discovering his architecture was a defining moment in my life. His buildings were surprising, joyous, fearless, timeless, and sexy, " she said, unable not to draw similar parallels as her gaze trawled along the perfect, taunt lines of Tariq's physique.

"I became obsessed," she said, deliberating turning her thoughts back to the safety of architecture. "I used to go traveling to see everything Lautner created, and I would bother the owners until they let me go inside."

"I like persistence in a woman," Tariq said.

She bit her lip."Unfortunately, I haven't met many men in my life who do. My dad also taught me how to build. It's ironic that despite all my accolades none of my designs have ever been built. I am nothing more than a paper architect." Her chin titled in defiance.

"Still—" her breath caught and sadness pooled in her voice, "—unlike Charlie and Zayed, I live to fight another day."

"I knew more about form and symmetry and building than most boys did," she added, as though trying to uplift herself.

No wonder she was so determined to work, he recalled. She forced her will to her career because that was how she avoided feeling pain. What right did he have to deny her the one area that brought her relief? He'd been selfish and that was about to change.

"Your father must have been very proud of you," he said.

He felt a kick of pleasure when her eyes brightened. She

wanted to make people proud. He admired that. He identified with that. It was a high standard in a world where people prefer to tear each other to shreds than offer a compliment.

“Yes, he was. I was so happy when he told me once that he’d been a fool to wish for a baby boy before I was born. I was so relieved when he told me that he had no idea then how fortunate he was to have a baby girl instead. I vowed then to show his faith in me was not misplaced."

"Your father was a brilliant man."

Her smile widened, and he found himself basking in the sensuous brilliance of her grin.

"My dad boasted to his friends that I was a planet in my own orbit—capable of cosmic courage and intergalactic innovation. He encouraged my creating fantastical shapes and forms and bringing them into reality. He bragged about my boldness, bravery, and competitiveness. I grew up believing I was powerful.” Her lips quivered at the memory, and he watched as the smile slid from her lips.

“It was a shock to discover when I tried to establish myself as an architect, that my peers didn’t believe that women had a place in architecture.”

Tariq’s sense of injustice flared.

“But having to fight harder has made me a better architect,” she said.

"I respect your determined optimism and warrior spirit,” Tariq said. “When others would have limped away defeated, you committed yourself to overcome obstacles and strove for continual improvement. You are a true warrior queen.”

She wanted to make the world a more beautiful, less brutal place. What option did he have then to help in her quest?

CHAPTER TWENTY-NINE

"Why did you never marry?" Tariq asked.

"I did marry. I married my job. I treat it with the same reverence, the same passion, the same devotion that a man treats his wife, and a woman treats her husband. No scratch that," she said quickly. "Not the same. Men quit their marriages. They cheat, they lie, and they betray."

Tariq chose silence over words, deliberately navigating the dangerous admission that he had not honoured his unspoken promises of never-ending love.

No matter how noble the cause, no matter how powerless he was to refuse the call to take the throne, he would not burden her with the truth that he was a reluctant King.

He would not tell her that when he learned his brother had abdicated that he went to his mother and wept. What sort of sovereign power puts his own needs first? What sort of a man puts the love of a woman first? What sort of a man puts his own selfish desires first? His brother's abdication and his own selfish pursuit of Charlie meant that Tariq's love for Melanie was an impossibility.

"Architecture would never do that to me, and I would never do that to architecture," she continued. "It is my love. It is my life. I am completely committed. That's why—" she chose her words carefully, '"that's why I can't be a mother."

Why did her attitude toward motherhood hurt so badly? And why couldn't she believe that a woman could work and raise a child? Why did their shared experiences growing up have to set the bar for their future? He wanted to ask her all of this, instead, he simply asked, "Why?"

"Because, like I've already said, if architecture doesn't kill you, you're no good. I never wanted to be mediocre. My mother was an extraordinarily gifted dancer. But it was only when she left that she flourished. When she walked out on me and my dad she told me she couldn't settle for less," her voice quivered.

"She told me that she had this fire inside and unless she flamed it she would be depressed. She told me that she would die. I grew up believing that if she had to look after me I would limit her life. I knew that unless I let her go I would be a rock tied around the waist of a drowning woman. How could I possibly ask any child I brought into this damaged world to make that call? How could I possibly give *my* child the love and devotion and the hundred percent commitment a child needs?"

Her eyes pooled with something Tariq thought looked like tears. He wanted to learn more, but he kept his confusion to himself. The whole night had been a confusing, bewildering, baffling mystery.

"How can I be a perfect mom and an extraordinary architect? The two are polar opposites. They're incompatible. Just like us. Somethings just aren't meant to go together, Tariq. Just like peanut butter and lettuce.

"You have some pretty strong beliefs, but what if you're wrong? What if you could have it all? "

"Impossible. A fairy tale. Complete make-believe. Women like me don't get to be CEO Cinderella. "

"A mind can't see what a heart won't look for," Tariq said.

"You're talking in riddles."

"Look at New Zealand."

"New Zealand?"

"It's a tiny country with big ideas. It's at the bottom of the world and yet it leads the way. It was the first country in the world to give women the right to drive their destiny when they gave women the right to vote. And they created history again, voting in the world's youngest female head of government in 2017. Jacinda Ardern took the most powerful seat in parliament at age 37. Within days or months of taking over the most powerful role in the nation, she fell pregnant. It may have thrown her, undoubtedly presented challenges, but she showed the world that *you can have it all.* A loving husband, a stay-at-home daddy, a fantastic career, the ability to influence—and be a loving mother."

Melanie frowned. "She has helpers."

"Yes, she does. She has an amazing husband, and a nanny —and she allows them to help. Have you ever considered that perhaps that's where you got it all wrong? You're so bloody-minded and singularly independent. It's a strength that I admire, but also a weakness. You won't ask for help and if it's offered you refuse it. But here's what I'm going to do. You need to put your stamp on architecture, you need to break through the boys club, you need to realise you can be a mother one day."

She blanched, making him feel as if he'd touched her nerves with the flame of a candle. She pressed her fingers to her lips and kept them there.

“I need a building to put my sanctuary on the world stage—and I need a mother for my brother's child. I was wrong when I said you shouldn’t work.”

There he’d said it.

Three words he never thought he would admit. It felt good. Dangerously good.

“I’m not a dinosaur—I don't believe women have to sacrifice their careers to be a mother,” he said. “But it's not what I believe, it's what you believe that's important. I want you to show me what you're capable of doing. I want you to put your architectural pen where your mouth is. So here's what I'm offering—a once in a lifetime chance to design a building with no barriers, no obstacles, no limits. Are you up for the challenge?”

CHAPTER THIRTY

"I want you to design a building that cannot be ignored," Tariq said.

"You do?"

"I want to create an education centre—a museum of sorts, a place to house all the activities related to my conservation project. Somewhere people, tourists, scientists, conservationists, media—a wide and diverse group of people can come under one roof and be united by a common cause. I want to attract tourists and diversity to boost my economy."

He hesitated, "So whatever you create needs to be, what was it you said you admired in Lautner's architecture? It needs to be fun. It needs to be uncompromising. It needs to be sexy—like you."

Was he playing with her? "I admire your vision. I'm in awe of what you've already achieved—the most ambitious conservation masterplan ever undertaken. I appreciate your faith in me. But I don't need your charity. Besides, what makes you think I'll be right for a project in Avana?" she protested looking around at the stoic, harsh lines of the palace's facade. "I don't think you're ready for me. And I know for a fact your people won't be."

"You are the perfect architect."

She liked the way he said *architect*. Not *woman architect*. Not because you are a female or any other annoying deference to her gender. She was an architect plain and simple. But he'd called her perfect. And that she knew was a lie. She was worse than imperfect. She was unworthy. Unworthy of his faith in her. Unworthy of his trust. Unworthy of his love.

"You know very little about me, Tariq." Her gaze swept the tiled floor. "I'm far from perfect."

"I may have been living in self-imposed exile, but I'm not uninformed. I've watched your career grow. I've read the accolades. I've marvelled and shared your father's pride when your designs have been nominated for awards. And I've been incensed when you've been judged unworthy and your designs rejected."

You rejected me. She lifted her gaze to his, as her lips formed a silent retort. *You abandoned me.*

She heard herself talking herself out of the commission and wished it could be different. It was a dream in all respects. A bottomless pit of money, a sponsor who held ultimate power and the purse-strings that provided the chance to create something dazzlingly innovative.

But she couldn't say yes. She couldn't stay. She couldn't risk his rejection, again. Fear and desire churned in her gut in a bitter battle.

"I'm not worthy," she repeated.

"What you think or what you believe doesn't factor into my decision. I've followed you for years. I know you. I know you have the fierce determination of a desert warrior queen. I know you possess a more formidable strength than a million vast sandstorms lined together. I know you have a greater stomach for controversy than all the camels in the world."

She wanted to say, 'No, Tariq, you don't know me. You don't know me at all. If you did you'd banish me from your kingdom and your life.' Instead she said, "You are too kind. You flatter me." She realised with alarm that his words had pierced the protective barriers she had so carefully constructed as a defence against his charms.

She felt the heat of his praise flush her cheeks, thaw her disappointed heart, melt into her hungry soul. "Flattery will not cause me to change my mind. The answer is no."

She would take her son and go.

"You misunderstand me, "Tariq growled. "This is a command. Not a request."

She got up to leave, but his hand pressed gently on her shoulders, forcing her back into her seat.

"Why are you looking so appalled? I thought you would be delighted. You can design anything your heart desires—you'll have an unlimited budget and I will not intervene. The only obstacle, if you choose to see him that way, is that you must balance work on this project with parenting, Salim. Can you do that?"

CHAPTER THIRTY-ONE

Parenting Salim.

Melanie pressed her fingers to her chest, trying to clear her heart. Trying to silence her old way of feeling. Her stress levels were soaring, her grip on control so loose she was afraid her whole life was going to slip from her reach.

Tariq had no idea of the pain that ripped through her. The aching void that no matter how much she denied existed was never fully sated by architecture. For so long she had denied how she truly felt.

Instead, she had filled every waking hour with architecture. She had convinced herself she could never do either one justice if she devoted herself purely to one. And now, he was insisting she do both.

And he still didn't know the truth.

She knew the only way to pull herself back together, the only way to gain some clarity, the only way to know what to do was not to be near him. She needed to be on her own so she could rebalance herself.

She craved distance, yet so wanted closeness. She

hungered for truth, yet she feared revelation. She thirsted for love, yet fear left her parched.

He was offering her a dream commission and instead of joy she felt despair.

Her voice was thickened with a toxic mix of regret, guilt, and shame. Her pain so acute she felt like vomiting.

She tried to run away but he locked his arm tightly around her waist. His eyes glittered. "What's wrong?"

She pushed against his powerful arms and freed herself from his grasp. "I'm not worthy," she cried. She ran. Ran as fast as her trembling legs would carry her. Ran deep into the night, wishing the darkness would swallow her grief.

Why the hell hadn't she left yesterday when she was still a free woman? Melanie ran towards the guesthouse and flung the door open and threw herself on her bed. She stared at the ceiling and recalled something she had read Karl Lagerfeld had said during his time at Chanel, 'Say yes to everything they ask you and everything they request and then do what you want.'

Men do that without blinking, Melanie thought. They think nothing of changing their minds and doing what they want. She didn't want to live with the sorrow or regret. The opportunity was too audacious to throw away like a penny.

Tariq had opened his considerable wealth to her. After years of battling, finally there would be no real constraints on what she could design, how long it was going to take to create, nor, more importantly, any cost limitations.

It was beyond her wildest dreams—and within her reach. The only person in her way was Melanie.

The Magic Melanie she always dreamed of becoming, created out of the planet innovative, industry-shaking designs. Designs with unparalleled superiority. And this was her chance. A chance to step into her essence. To break the chains of her identity. To create a concept, a narrative, so revolutionary it would change everything.

She lay back against the soft sheets and sunk into the floaty, cloud-like linen. Finally, freed of constraints and allowed to create something to her own designs she had two choices. Keep putting a hand-break on her past, or press her foot on the accelerator and speed ahead.

She gazed over at the orchids artfully arranged beside her bed, draped with little beaded pearl lights. Inspiration struck as she gazed into their deep magenta centre. Magenta, the colour of universal harmony and emotional balance.Magenta the symbol of universal love at its highest level. Magenta, the colour that promotes compassion, kindness, and cooperation and encourages a sense of self-respect and contentment in those who use it.

Yes, the path was dazzlingly clear. She wanted this. She wanted to create architecture that was actually a piece of floral artistry. She wanted to make Tariq proud.

And Tariq would love it. She was certain of that. Magenta, the colour of self-respect, told her that. If he loved it so much, when she at last found the perfect time to tell him the truth, he might even find it in his heart to forgive her.

She couldn't turn back the time that had escaped them, but she could try, in the only way she knew how, to make up for those missing years.

CHAPTER THIRTY-TWO

Melanie was too excited to sleep and she decided to visit Salim and read him another story. A bedtime story. He still hadn't woken from his coma, but the more she read to him, the more she felt she was making up for all those nights she hadn't been there to read or kiss him to sleep.

She plucked two orchids from the stem, and tucked one behind her ear, and carried the other to place by Salim's bed.

Every day was like nighttime for Salim, she thought, as she entered the hospital room. She watched the gentle rise and fall of his tiny chest. She placed the orchid by his head, hoping the sweet perfume would work some magic alchemy and stir him from his slumber.

And then did something she hadn't done in years. She knelt on the prayer rug Tariq had placed in the room, and prayed.

"Dear God, Please forgive me my sins. Please forgive me my wrongs. Please forgive me my pride. Please help me make right the wrongs of my past. Please heal my son. Please bring him back to life. Please help me use my gifts in a way I may serve this world. Please help me fulfil the purpose of life, to bring you joy."

She didn't know if Tariq would ever forgive her of her sins. She would never know how different things might have been had she given up working and raised her son.

She couldn't undo time. She had done the best she could. Perhaps one day Tariq and the people of Avana would understand. Perhaps one day she would forgive herself.

But for now, she just wanted to fill Salim's life with special moments.

* * *

She told Tariq that she would accept his offer, and filled the days, as she waited for the things she needed to complete her work to arrive, visiting her son.

Sitting with Salim for hours every day she began to read to him the stories which as a child she used to love.

Fun stories by Dr. Suess and other books her father had read to her as a child. She knew no matter how much she tried those three years would always be missing. But she loved Salim more than he would ever understand. Perhaps when he woke and his memory returned, or perhaps later, when he was a young man, he may not be as forgiving. But right now she counted her blessings.

And she knew that one day what she would finally create would sustain Salim and Tariq for years to come and hopefully fill them with a sense of pride at her lasting legacy.

It was her gift for them. Her architecture had always been inspired by her son. Without the knowledge he was alive she never would have tried so hard.

* * *

"You did this for me?"

Melanie drew a ragged breath. It was as though Tariq had transported her architecture studio and recreated it in the kingdom of Avana. At one end of the huge light-filled room was her workstation. Everything she needed was there—a stand-up desk, Apple computers, several big drawing boards on stands made of round metal tube with a hydraulic lift for height adjustment. Even her beloved pens, and sketchbooks.

And in the corner of the room, where she could easily keep an eye on her son when he finally awoke, and her son could keep an eye on her, was the most adorable playpen. It was a fairytale fortress that would awaken and inspire any creativity Salim may hopefully have inherited from his mother.

"No," he said gruffly, "I did it for me. Do not mistake my furnishing of your study for anything more than that—a place for you to work, and care for the boy at the same time."

He'd been cool with her since she had rebuked him, and while it hurt, for now it suited her perfectly. She needed to focus on the formidable challenge she had set herself.

Melanie carefully studied the placement of everything. For someone with his aloof coolness, he had gone to considerable effort to add an unexpected touch of homeliness. Her paintings, drawings, sculptural pieces, and other hand-crafts were everywhere. Patiently waiting, dancing, embracing her—giving off pulses of visual energy.

Tears blurred her eyes, and she quickly turned to look at the library of books lining the far end of what was now her studio. She walked toward the ceiling-high bookcases and ran her fingers along the spine of several of the many hundreds of architecture and design books lining the walls.

Her eyes trailed over the large volumes on artists she esteemed. CY Twombly, Mark Rothko, Frank Lloyd Wright, John Lautner and her most inspirational muse—Dame Zaha Hadid. Her eyes watered as she studied the spines and saw the names of the architects she had told Tariq that had so inspired and influenced her work.

"Gosh, I don't know what to say," she said turning to him. "You're a very resourceful man," she said, looking at the display of architectural models placed on the shelves running along the inner wall. "Where did you get these? They're iconic."

His unreadable expression didn't change. "I had them flown in."

Despite his stiff facade, she noticed the lift of pleasure in his voice. He had enjoyed making her happy. And she knew it.

It made Melanie wonder how different all their lives might have been. She and Tariq and their son, working and living together, enriching, not destroying, each others lives. All this time, could she have successfully been a working wife and mother? Had she been wrong to listen to her mother?

CHAPTER THIRTY-THREE

She shoved her thoughts to the back of her mind. Playing happy families successfully might not have happened anyway. Dreams only came true in the Grimm's fairytales she read to Salim.

She turned her focus to her new working environment. On the opposite end to her work area was an enclosed, mosaic courtyard with a fountain she could look out onto when her mind needed refreshing. Near the window, looking out across the fountain were two plump leather seats and a table to take refreshments.

Tariq gestured her to one of these seats, then excused himself to speak to his cousin who was waiting outside. She could hear them making plans for Zayed's burial.

Melanie was glad for the opportunity to sit down and be alone with her memories.

Her gaze drifted beyond the courtyard where the men and women of Avana were going about their everyday lives. Enjoying life, as they invariably did, regardless of death, births, marriages—and divorces.

An underlying sense of panic started churning through her

stomach again. She didn't want to bring up her child alone. She remembered how hard it had been without a helpmate when Salim was born. Tariq's brother and her sister had been so kind and generous, taking him into their hearts and lives.

Her thought drifted back over the past three years. Melanie had to acknowledge her life had become rather flat and routine. Surely every career had its highs and lows. It was just that she never had anyone to share the highs with and lately the lows had…well the lows had just become lower.

It was a matter of working harder, being committed, trying to be as good as she could be. She didn't understand why is was so difficult. Wasn't it supposed to be easier with no children and no husband? Why had it gone so wrong?

The sound of the studio door opening snapped her mind to the immediate present. Tariq stood in the doorway. He looked so big and powerful, a boulder to lean on, and Melanie ached for the support that his protection seemed to offer.

Yet she knew that she couldn't afford to let Tariq get close to her. It could only confuse everything far more than it was already confused.

Tariq didn't know that he had left her pregnant three years ago. He knew nothing of the son she had given birth to nine months after his brother had abdicated.

He had married another woman. And she had come to believe that he wouldn't want to know, long before she had given Salim up to her sister to raise.

Whether that was really true or not, it was not possible to change the course of events that had occurred. Charlotte and Zayed had pretended to everyone that Salim was their natural-born child, only Melanie knew the truth.

Melanie knew Salim had been legally adopted by them. To all intents and purposes, Zayed was Salim's father. Tariq was Salim's uncle. Charlotte was his mother, and Melanie was his aunt. It was best for everyone if it stayed that way. Wasn't it? For now, anyway.

Nevertheless, Melanie allowed herself the luxury of really studying Tariq for the few seconds it took him to cross the floor of the studio, noting the likenesses to her son. *Their son.*

Deeply dark golden eyes, although Salim's irises were tinged with blue and green, and Tariq's hazel brown. The thick tousled hair was a strikingly similar shade of raven black. Salim's upper lips were softer, and fuller, more like hers, and the shape of his face rounder, less hard-boned and chiseled. Perhaps as Salim grew into a young man, his jawline would firm into the same determined, authoritative set as his father's.

Her gaze drifted to the stylish leather shoes on Tariq's feet. Feet she knew had a longer second toe on the left foot than the big one. The mark of a genius Tariq had laughingly told her. Leonardo da Vinci had one too, and Tariq was the cleverest in his age group at University where they studied. Would Salim inherit both their gifts? What a formidable, special young man he would grow to be.

"Lani…"

She lifted her gaze. Lani, the name he had called her when they first met.

"Would you like coffee brought in?"

She shook her head.

"Is there anything else you need?"

Where could she begin?

"No," she said, softly, noticing the trace of sadness in her voice. "I'm grateful for this opportunity," she said, turning her focus away from personal thoughts to the professional role for which he was employing her. "I have everything I want. I don't want to be any trouble."

"I would never consider you trouble," he said seriously.

She grimaced. That's what you think now. You will not always think that way.

"You know what I mean. I don't intend to get in your way," she said.

"If I can be of help to you, at any time, please call. I'll do all I can for you," he assured her.

She could see the deep sincerity in his eyes, and it hurt. Unbearably.

Where were you when I needed you? She cried in silent anguish.

CHAPTER THIRTY-FOUR

"Why did you tell Tariq about my drawings," Melanie said, when she caught up with Latifa again.

"Do you not have a dress? Are you a woman or not?" Latifa said, staring with dismay at her shirt, and pants.

"I could ask you the same thing," Melanie shot back, gesturing to her skinny jeans, sneakers and T-shirt.

Latifa grinned, "I'm not trying to claim a Sheikh—whereas, you are."

"I'm not."

Latifa shrugged. "And that's why I told my brother. Tariq has become hard. He fears losing people he loves. I want to change that. You're good for him."

"Tariq doesn't trust me. No one here does."

"Trust has to be earned and should come only after the passage of time. But there is something you can do to ease the process. Are you interested in learning our ways?" Latifa asked.

"Of course. I told Tariq that when I arrived. Your culture has always entranced me. I love the history, the art—"

"Do you love to dance?"

"Dance? With my two left feet?"

Latifa laughed. "It helps to have two feet when you are belly dancing."

"I'm a young, white, middle class, chair-dweller. There's no way I could coordinate my body parts to create some vague impression of belly dancing."

"I will teach you."

"Impossible. I'll make a fool of myself."

"Were you good at architecture when you first started?" Latifa asked.

"Of course not."

"But you had a desire?"

"Yes."

"And you wanted to win?"

"Yes. I wanted to be the best."

"And you gave architecture your heart?"

"I gave architecture my life."

"And my brother? Is there room in your life for my brother? Will you give him your heart?"

"He doesn't want it."

"He doesn't realise what he needs. What he needs is the freedom to let go of the past. You do too. Freedom lives on the edge of your comfort zone. Are you willing to risk, are you willing to learn, are you willing to grow?"

Melanie nodded.

"Then I will teach you. I will teach you how to penetrate his walls. I will teach you how to smash through his defences. I will teach you how to dance your way into his heart so that he will never be satisfied until he claims you as his and only his."

"I don't want to be possessed," Melanie said, stiffening.

"Possession in the East does not mean what it does in the

West," Latifa said. "I have watched you. Your energy is that of a warrior, masculine, firm, purposeful and unyielding. It is not a criticism. I know better than most how difficult it is to be a woman in this world. But you risk becoming brittle. Be like water, which is fluid and soft and yielding. In time, water will overcome rock which is rigid and hard. What is softer is stronger."

Melanie's eyes glazed in a hypnotic trance as Latifa began to dance."You make it look so airy and effortless," Melanie said.

'Trust me, it was not always so. The spine gets freer, and energy flows more easily after practicing belly dance isolations for a month or two."

Melanie looked at her dubiously.

"When was the last time you moved your ribcage sideways or in a circle?" Latifa asked.

Melanie looked blankly, suddenly aware of just how rigid her body was. She pressed her hand to her stomach, achingly aware of how separate her body was from her mind. Her belly suddenly felt heavy. She had cut off the very place she had carried Tariq's baby from her reality.

"All this energy flowing up and down the spine," Latifa said, running her palm down the length of Melanie's body, "through these chakras or energy centers of the body, can release lots of pent-up emotional or mental material."

Her eyes drifted from Melanie's stomach up to her eyes. "Women who stick with belly dancing really open up. They become freer, as though a great burden has been lifted, an aching wound healed."

"That easy, huh?" Melanie, said, dubiously.

"Learning to dance was life-changing for me. It came when I really needed it. I was in a healing crisis, realising that I needed to release old sadness as well as heal a back so messed up that my chiropractor said it was an example of how 'God makes mistakes!' He knew as well as I did that it was my father who made the mistake."

Melanie listened as Latfia shared her story of how she had been imprisoned and tortured by her father. It was horrifying. Beyond horrifying. It was appalling and her heart went out to her for how she had suffered.

"What father does that to his daughter?"

Latifa shrugged. "An evil one. He was who he was. I was glad he died. And I was glad that I found a way to heal. Most every morning, I would dance and it would dispel my habitual depression and allow my higher, brighter spirit to express itself. My stiff, aching back normally restricted my body's movements, but the gentle undulations of 'the dance' allowed my body to move in a joyful expression of life. And it healed me emotionally and physically. As a part of a daily practice of meditation, prayer, and good nutrition, belly dance helped me re-create a damaged body and psyche."

"It sounds like a miracle cure," Melanie said.

"Yes, as time went on, my pain lessened until I was totally free of it. I came to embody more of the joyful being that is my higher self, my true self. Belly dance was my physical therapy and my emotional therapy. It was my connection with the Goddess energies flowing from earth to me and from me into the world. It helped the kundalini to flow fluidly through my body," Latifa said.

"It's a pretty compelling story. Inspiring, " Melanie said, respect deepening for the unruly princess.

"Tariq has been more of a father to me than our father was. I owe him my life. The experience closed my heart to relationships but it doesn't have to be a life sentence for my brother. "

"I'm not sure what I can do."

"Dance changes you. It changes your life because when you do it you feel differently. You find self-acceptance and you stop worrying so much about how others see you. Others may feel envious that you are so free and able to have this outlet. It's a blessing to be able to move and glide across a floor. It's a way to celebrate life. It's a way to celebrate you. A way to break free of your past, free of your role, free of your carefully cultivated identity. It's a way to show Tariq who you really are and who you really can be. That's what you can do."

CHAPTER THIRTY-FIVE

It was late and Melanie had put in a long time balancing work, time with Salim, and sneaking in her belly dancing classes with Latifa. Latifa was right. It was freeing and it did make her feel better about her body.

She been puzzling over her designs when she heard the most hypnotic musical sound. Intrigued she followed the trail of notes like bread crumbs and was guided to Salim's hospital room.

"Sweet dreams dear boy," Tariq whispered as he lifted the mouthpiece from his lips and placed the saxophone back in its protective case.

She stood in the doorway, her feet riveted to the floor, completely struck by what she heard and what she saw. "Don't stop," she said, quietly. "It's so hauntingly beautiful. I didn't know you played."

"Clutching at notes," he said. "Nothing else is stirring the child. I don't want him to spend his life like this."

"No," she said. "Neither do I."

"Please play a little more," she said, going to Salim's side.

"I'm a little creaky. I haven't played since—" he paused,

and lifted the instrument from the case again. "Not since my mother left."

They stood together, united in sympathetic understanding.

"I thought, well, you know I'm not much good at saying how I feel. Some people consider the saxophone to be the instrument most resembling the human voice. I thought I could reach him that way."

He took a deep breath and began to play. It was a bright sound, so unlike his own voice. The timbre of hopefulness, healing, and love. Who would have thought an instrument could be so versatile she thought, as she stroked Salim's hair.

His eyelids began to flutter and she leaned closer. Disbelieving and believing at the same time. His long lashes lifted slowly.

"He's awake," she cried. "Look he's opening his eyes."

Tariq pressed the saxophone to his lips, as though afraid, that like a snake charmer, if he no longer played there would no longer by the magic that had woken the boy from his slumber.

Salim looked around, blinking rapidly as though struggling to focus.

"Nurse! Nurse!" Melanie called, over the plaintive overtones saturating the room.

"Don't worry," the nurse said, checking the boy as she responded to Melanie's startled cry. "It's normal for him to look disorientated. On television, it seems like someone in a coma wakes up right away, looks around, and is able to think and talk normally. But in real life, this rarely happens. When coming out of a coma, he will probably be confused and only slowly respond to what's going on. It will take time for him to start feeling better."

"And his brain?" Tariq said, as he put his instrument down and went to Salim's side.

"Whether someone fully returns to normal after being in a coma depends on what caused the coma and how badly the brain may have been hurt. Sometimes people who come out of comas are just as they were before. They can remember what happened to them before the coma and can do everything they used to do."

"Like talk?"

"It's too early to tell. He may need therapy to relearn basic things like tying his shoes, eating with a fork or spoon, or learning to walk all over again. He may also have problems with speaking or remembering things. Over time and with the help of therapists, however, many people who have been in a coma can make a lot of progress. They may not be exactly like they were before the coma, but they can do many things and enjoy life with their family."

"Mommy," Salim cried.

Melanie fought back tears. Mommy the word she never thought she'd even live to hear.

"Daddy," he added.

Relief washed over her. At least the boy has misrecognised them both. He thought she was Charlie and Tariq was Zayed. Or had he? Because Melanie had been studying up on Arabic philosophy, she wondered if it was possible that the boy recognised them both on some soul level.

She pressed her palm to her eyes. She didn't know what to think. She had known the day would come when he awoke, but now that it was here she was totally, absolutely, blindly unprepared.

"We're not your daddy and mommy," Tariq said softly.

Melanie threw him a contemptuous look.

"Now may not be the best time to tell the boy the truth," the nurse said. "Give the boy time. Give yourselves time," she said, turning to them both. "Sometimes the kindest thing you can do for a person is to maintain a sacred silence. Sometimes, it's better not to know the truth."

She turned to Salim and adjusted his bandages. "Sometimes a severe injury to the head hurts the brain, or he may have had a seizure. We'll never know what really happened that night of the accident. He shows no obvious injuries. But when one of these things happens, it can mess up how the brain's cells work. This can hurt the parts of the brain that affects memory and their ability to recall things accurately."

Melanie prayed inwardly. I hope he's a little fighter—like his dad.

* * *

Whether it was the prayer or purely the fact he had the strength of a little lion, Salim made a rapid recovery. The speed of which amazed everyone. It seemed that his memory was still compromised, and he kept referring to Tariq and Melanie as daddy and mommy.

If Melanie was honest, it was what she had always hoped for. Perhaps the nurse was right. Maybe it wouldn't hurt if they allowed him to believe what he wanted to believe. She told herself it wasn't hurting anyone. In fact, just the opposite.

CHAPTER THIRTY-SIX

Melanie stared at the blank sheet of paper, willing inspiration to strike, but nothing came. Forcing herself to create something, anything, she set her ruler to the page and drew a faint, half-hearted series of lines.

Lines!

She hated lines, but there they were, she thought glumly, staring at the harsh sharp angles and dislocated spaces.

Despairingly, she looked up. From the window she could see Salim playing in the garden, near the fountain chortling with delight while holding a wriggling worm in his hand for the first time.

She watched as he ran toward the small flight of stone steps leading past the sensuous rhythm of tropical plants toward the meditation garden. A smile creased her lips as she savoured the inspiring innocence of his perception, endlessly fascinated with jumping off the same step over and over.

Melanie briefly returned her focus to her drawing board, then looked up again, marvelling at her child's capacity for wonder.

Joy.

The word fluttered to her lips. That was what was missing from her life. Was it possible that rather than distract her from her work, her son could lift her vision higher? Could he help her reclaim the capacity for joy she had felt as a child, before she was buried under a maelstrom of criticism and became her disillusioned, adult-self?

In a frenzy of activity she picked up her pencils. Suddenly, it was so clear to her. When our eyes are tired, the world appears bleak. When our hearts are jaded and desensitised, the world becomes colourless and flat. The sensitive, mindful heart perceives value and worth in all things. It does not rely upon drama or intensity to feel awake and alive; but draws upon receptivity, stillness, and a present-moment wholeheartedness.

With flourishing, playful sweeps across the paper she reworked her drawings, adding more liberated imaginative forms. Forms she knew would be unacceptable to major corporate clients. Her free-form sweeps went on the attack destroying the stronghold of rectilinear design which had crept back into her drawings.

She had been wounded by the officials who had rejected her concept for the community library. But now she felt distinctly empowered. Geometry and science, inspired by the curiosity of her son, were once again her prime movers.

"Jump, Jump, Jump," she encouraged herself, "Go ahead and jump, stop holding back," she shouted out loud, urging her designs to break all known constraint.

Jump, jump, jump sprang her pencil as Melanie sketched in a sweep of arching steps in a crescendo of *stellato* movements.

The effect was dazzling. Now rather than purely cognitive and applied as a design imposed from the outside world she was creating organically, just like life and nature, from within.

Her pulse raced. The design emerged perfectly formed. Like a baby at last springing forth from its protective, nourishing slumber, the vanguard of a new holistic architecture.

Down she dived, plunging deeper and deeper into the world of spiritual expression and organic form where the wonder and the essential beauty of the natural world merged seamlessly with the essential practical needs of economy, efficiency, and conservation.

She felt restless, drawing with an energy almost beyond her. It was as though she was possessed by a force not quite her own. She sweated in the dry heat of the room and registered the scratch of her pen as she scrawled her design as fast as she could.

Seized by the Muse her design took on a life and vitality of its own. A breaking wave, she thought, flourishing a series of curvaceous lines to form the roofline.

"What is now coming is the Breaking Wave, a new architecture that expresses the union of organic inspiration and truly sustainable design," she said in a moment of joyful resonance. "Yes! Yes! Yes! This is who I am." she cried as she threw down her pen. She pushed back from her standup desk, ran to the door and skipped outside.

"I love you! I love you! I love you!" she cried, sweeping her son into her arms and sprinkling kisses on his giggling face.

He wrapped his arms around her neck, and curved his body into hers, fusing them as one. His little legs swung back and forth as she nuzzled her neck into his. "Thank you! Thank you! Thank you! You have given me back my life. You have given me back my joy. You have given me back my soul, Salim"

CHAPTER THIRTY-SEVEN

Melanie was seated on a high stool at her desk amongst the busy clutter. The once clear white surface was crammed with the paraphernalia of creativity, trays of tube colours, bowls of brushes and drawing implements. The walls Tariq had left so pristine were now festooned with drawings, paintings, and sketches. But rather than irritate him her busy productivity inspired him.

What did it matter if the place was a mess, Tariq told himself as a spotlight of searing sun ran drew a radiant golden line across her hair, and trailed along her face. In deep concentration Melanie reviewed the photographs of her past work.

As he watched her it struck him what a beautiful, yet lonely woman she was. Immersed in her world of architecture, he now understood why she had deliberately isolated herself. Had he not done the same thing by shunning humanity? He had immersed himself in his animal kingdom and she in her bricks and mortar.

Rather than want to retreat, the intensity with which she

conducted her work stirred his curiosity and evoked a solid, reassuring presence. It was as unsettling as it was exciting.

He watched as she picked up her pen and swept it across her sketchpad in a series of swooping curves. Her movements were confident, strong, yet economical. Her mood so purposeful and business-like.

Tariq's eyes grew hot, a contrast to the weight crushing his lungs. This moment, this beautiful moment, was killing his resolve never to again marry.

He thought she would be more…well…he didn't really know what he thought. He felt confused by the powerful push-pull of desire coursing through his loins and his default habit of wanting to run. He wanted her. He wanted the vitality, the rebelliousness that she possessed. And yet he had grown used to his self-reliant sanctuary.

As though conscious of his lingering gaze Melanie looked up. "You startled me," she said. "How long have you been there?"

Her eyes widened into beautiful pools, stirring his libido. She was like no other woman he had ever met, sure but a hundred-times more dangerous. She awoke a dangerous desire to claim her as his own.

"What are you proudest of?" Tariq asked, picking up one of the photos of her work.

"That somehow, through sheer force of will, and luck, and circumstance, I have managed to eke out a living from the thing that I do best," she said.

"But I will never be satisfied being called a paper architect," she said, with a fierce vulnerability that unsettled him.

"If I had a euro for every time someone told me my plans were unbuildable, I'd be rich enough to build them myself. For years, my designs struggled to move beyond the sketch phrase and be transformed into bricks and mortar. My grand design," she said, "Is to be renown for building the unbuildable."

"You shall not have to wait long," he said, with the fierce dynamism which had cemented his reputation as a king of kings.

She regarded him dubiously. "I'm not sure your people will be as assured as you when they discover what I have created. Experience has taught me that my designs will catch people off guard. It won't surprise me if they say that I'm too independent and flamboyant to be taken seriously."

"That is why I commissioned you. That and your penchant for experimentation. Your refusal to compromise your concepts or designs. The force of your convictions that you will not be restrained by practical constraints or technology. I want what others fear. I want your swooping, curved, futuristic buildings. I want your structurally intricate layered forms. I want to support everything your competitors hold sacrosanct—and oppose. There is beauty in opposition," Tariq said.

"Your designs don't just do away with boundaries; your flamboyant buildings arguably helped to popularise and thus glamorise architecture into something for onlookers to enjoy, rather than merely utilise. This is why I want you."

He wondered if Melanie could sense he could feel the scorching heat of her skin and the rapid flutter of her heart. He wondered if she could feel his own growing excitement.

"Want me?" she forced her voice to a nonchalant crawl.

"Your designs," he said, tampering down the need to tell her how he really felt.

Was that disappointment he sensed in the downward curve of those fine lips? Was that sadness he registered in the pooling of her eyes? Was that feigned detachment he saw as she thrust back her slim shoulders?

"Tomorrow we leave on an overnight safari. I want you to truly absorb the surroundings. The beauty of the desert by day and by night." He blurted, wondering what on earth had possessed him to expose himself to temptation.

"Night?" she stammered.

"You have no need to fear—not in that way. I will not impose myself upon you again."

CHAPTER THIRTY-EIGHT

The wake of Tariq's departure emphasised the empty void. Melanie threw a wash of ink over her drawing pad, obliterating any trace of the drawing she had sketched earlier. She would rather die than be claimed by a sheikh who didn't want her.

Stupid woman, she muttered, glancing down where the happy family she had rendered in coloured pencils had once run across the paper so joyfully. What a giant mess, she thought as she looked down at the black puddle submerging Tariq, Salim, and Melanie.

She glanced out the window as she sat alone in her studio.

Melanie had spent her life surrounded by people and yet alone. Escaping into her world of architecture she had convinced herself that buildings were her friends. She had always imagined that paradise would be living out her days locked in her studio, immersed in an architectural library. Tariq had granted that wish.

And now, as she sat, in the solemn quiet she realised she had spent her life in poverty. Architecture was not the companion she truly needed, architecture could not love her back. She could not interact with her designs like the two ladies she saw together near the fountain in the courtyard. Laughing to each other, chuckling as they volleyed stories about their husbands, their children, and their lives.

No, she thought, turning her gaze to the models of buildings she had designed, architecture always lay silent in the background.

She thought of Tariq and their verbal spas. He was a worthy opponent, mentally sharp, formidably intelligent, supremely cultured and learned. Her body hummed with anticipation as she thought of his potent physicality. No, architecture would never give her that arousal.

And while part of her accepted Tariq would never be hers, part of her relished the thought of experiencing the heated thrill of his body writhing on top of hers in forbidden seduction.

Yes, he wanted to play. But none of the games she knew she could win. The game he wanted to play was far, far more dangerous. He wanted to play with fire. And she did too. She knew he was denying his own need when he said he would not impose upon her. He wanted her every bit as much as she wanted him. She wanted to kiss his sensuous mouth, strip off the *dishdasha* that clung to his powerful pecs and seek oblivion in the most basic way known to any woman who had spent years not being touched by the man she had always loved.

And she wanted to do it again and again until her mind was wiped of everything that made her feel ashamed. Except him. Until she forgot the burden she carried in her heart. Until the pain of remembering the secret she kept hidden was buried beneath orgasmic joy.

So, he wanted to play overnight safari. It would be the perfect night to enchant him with her secret sauce of seduction. Why not? Besides, it was Latifa's idea to weave a spell around her emotionally frozen brother, and nothing else had worked. Nothing else had helped heal the divide between them. All she hoped, was that she didn't trip over her two left feet.

CHAPTER THIRTY-NINE

She needn't have worried about being left on her own with the desert warrior. As it turned out, it was a special occasion and a whole caravan of locals, including ancient tribesmen, were coming together to celebrate in the desert.

A wave of emotion crashed through her belly. On the one hand, she was terrified of performing in front of so many people. On the other, she was pleased to have the opportunity to show Tariq's people how much importance and how much effort she was prepared to put into learning and embracing their ancient customs.

Against a backdrop lit by torches and strewn with carpets and cushions, the guests gathered feasted on mezze, barbecue fare, wood-fired bread, and sticky sweets.

The setting sun glowed indolently, a giant fiery-red and violet blaze in the dusty haze. The alluring scent of jasmine, amber, musk, and *oud* perfumed the air. With Latifa's expert help, everything was so carefully curated.

* * *

Tariq had returned from helping the men set up camp for the night when he found her centre-stage in front of an admiring audience.

What a beauty she was. Sensual and seductive and mesmerising, he thought as he watched, entranced by the surprising apparition writhing before his hungry eyes.

Melanie ground her hips in tiny staccato movements, then tossed her head, arching and lowering her body dramatically toward the giant antique Persian rug.

A jet-black river of hair, streaked with henna cascaded down her voluptuous breasts. Oblivious to the admiring crowd, Tariq followed the line of her glistening body. His eyes riveted to her slim ankles entwined with sparkling circles of diamonds, rubies and sapphires.

He never suspected for a moment she was capable of dancing, let alone capturing the heart of Avana culture so perfectly.

The drumming of the Arabic music pulsed through his mind, sending his thoughts soaring. Melanie rose slowly pinning her gaze to his, drawing him to her with hypnotic kohl-rimmed eyes, as though sensing his intoxication.

The smudgy band of black eyeliner was so perfect on her giant, gorgeous eyes, he was powerless to look away. Did she know that the scent of rose, jasmine and spicy amber had the mystical power to wash away almost anything—even his resolve?

She lowered her gaze in feigned piety, pretending to be oblivious to the power she held over him as her body flowed in continuous sinuous movements. She rolled and twisted her hips, the rocked them vertically, drawing his attention to her beautiful stomach.

His gaze drifted to the tiny emerald nestled against the tiny knot of her belly button. He found himself fantasising about what a fantastic mother she would make. He fantasied about making love to her. He fantasied about impregnating her with his royal seed. He fantasied about cutting the umbilical cord and holding their child. No matter how he tried to dislodge the thought he could not get her out of his head.

A pearl of tiny bells brought him back from his reverie. His attention drifted to the little golden bells which clung to the vibrant rouge red silk of Melanie's flowing skirt sitting low on her hips.

Her tight-fitting brassiere amplified the full swell of her breasts, which billowed over her generous cleavage. She wore a long shimmering gold cape that fluttered across the floor as she danced with the grace of a butterfly. She grasped the edges of the silk in her sensuous fingers and drew the cape around her, as she pirouetted in graceful circles.

Then, still grasping the edge she raised the cape in the air like the wings of the ancient goddess Isis. The torchlights around the camp arched and flickered, and the setting sun, now soft and pink, bounced off the fabric, creating glints of light that mimicked the stars. His heart danced in unison at the sight of her magical display.

Around her neck she wore expensive jewels. But it was her face and the look of pure joy that was priceless. She was shining, brilliant, dazzling and iridescent. She whirled and whirled, turning around and around and around, her hair tumbling seductively down her back, lost in a trance, oblivious to the desire she was eliciting.

With the figure of Venus, a flaming mane of dense henna-coloured hair, feline-green eyes and an exceptionally beautiful face, she was a magnet he felt powerless to resist.

Beauty shone forth from her soul, her ego, the mask of masculine-bravado she wore to protect herself, surrendered to the freedom the dance elicited. She was in her essence and he loved her.

Tariq could not tear his eyes from her. She was smiling, laughing, her hips gyrating, her delicious bottom wiggling, rolling back and forth causing the beaded jewels of her dress to send a prism of light splaying into the crowd.

Tariq studied the faces of his people who had gathered to watch her, beneath the velvet dark sky, studded with diamond-like stars in the middle of the desert. An old woman sat smiling, a tear trickling down her cheek. Another clapped, following the rhythmic beat of the music. An old man sat silently, nodding his appreciation. Two young girls, in traditional dress, held their iPhones in front of their faces, giggling as they recorded Melanie's sultry dance.

She exuded the kind of naturally warm and approachable sex appeal that attracted the opposite sex in droves. Men wanted to bed her, and women wanted to be her.

Had it not been for Melanie's modest assessment of her considerable assets and her innate kindness, Tariq was convinced the crowd would have been consumed with envy or disdain. But Tariq saw the admiration in their eyes, the acceptance. He knew she had won their hearts.

She belonged.

He suddenly realised how much he wanted her to himself. He imagined carrying her to his tent, lifting the tumbling cascade of curls that writhed down her back, and pulling the fabric bow of her sequinned brassiere so that her ample breasts feel free into his waiting palms.

He would lower his lips to her nipples and kiss her again and again, parting her skirt as he did so, in readiness to savour that sweetest of nectars, the honeyed liqueur which flowed from her.

He wanted all of her now, but instead had to curb his

appetite. How could he deny his people this rare pleasure? But more importantly, how could he deny Melanie her chance to shine?

He forced his mind from his desire to claim her and make love to her under the endless sky. Pinning his thoughts to the present he studied her hands as she danced. They were so expressive, he thought, as she pinched her sensuous fingers slightly, speaking loudly with no words, as she lifted them into the air in a twirling river of seduction.

Melanie ran her hands through her hair, tossed her head, sending a sexy tumble of glistening hair down her spine and beckoned him with her teasing smile.

She bunched her locks, clasping them above her head momentarily, as she danced toward him, thrusting her pelvis forward, gyrating her hips, causing the ribbon of silk covering her womanhood to part seductively.

He caught the briefest glimpse of that forbidden part of her veiled in fine silk. Her thighs glistened, the profile of her firm buttocks taunting him mercilessly.

Every cell in his body awakened and rejoiced.

She laughed, fully aware of his discomfort, and mouthed the words of the song as she sang along with the music. Then tossed her head from side to side in a rhythmic wave. Again and again. Her hair flying through the air. Then she picked up a golden sabre. She grazed it upon her thigh, then lifted it to her throat.

A prism of light sauntered along the blade, then glinted dangerously along the sharpest edge. A knife could cut, hurt, and kill; but it could also prune, heal, and save lives. It could cut an umbilical cord and bring a child into the world.

His sister Latifa had taught him the eastern chakra system. Melanie was sending him a clear message. The choice was his. Did he possess the wisdom, faith, purification, and ability to trust? Or was he going to mutilate their love with his continued suspicion?

He wanted to call out to her, ‘My choice is made,’ but as magically as she appeared, she disappeared into the crowd.

Where was she going and why was she leaving so soon?

CHAPTER FORTY

The sandstorm approached so gracefully, that at first Melanie didn't register the threat. She had been on such a euphoric high following her dance, she wanted to cool off. And she wanted to enjoy the peace of the desert and be alone with her conflicting thoughts.

She glanced at the horizon as the cloud of dust grew thicker. Should she be worried, she wondered? It spiralled with increasing urgency, like some ominous dance, covering everything in a dusty haze until everything in the distance was buried.

Were it not so menacing it would be beautiful Melanie thought, momentarily beguiled. Billowing clouds of sand, infused with champagne golds, rose pinks, and edged with creamy white, set perfectly against a moody night sky.

"Quickly. Ride with me on Johara," Tariq said, his tone rough with urgency, as he jumped from the horse.

Hitching up the red plumes of her silk skirt, she thrust her foot in his hand and allowed him to heave her onto the back of the horse. She clung to his waist as he mounted the desert stallion and pressed her head against his powerful shoulders.

She shuddered and clenched her fingers more firmly around his stomach as a wall of cloud rolled across the horizon, looking back at the giant tsunami, devouring everything in its wake.

"Here it comes," she yelled. "Oh my God, Tariq here it comes. It's insane," she said, as a large whooshing roar filled the air.

"Cover your mouth," Tariq yelled, "The sand is dangerous. If you swallow too much you could die."

"Die!" She didn't want to die. She didn't want to leave her son. She didn't want to lose the men she loved.

She extracted an arm from around his waist and wound the gold cape several times around her face, leaving the tiniest gap through which to breathe.

As they approached the tented city Tariq grabbed the reins and drew the horse to a stop.

Hamad hastened to grab the reins, as Tariq leaped to the hot sand. Tariq lifted her from the horse and ran with her in his arms, into the tent.

"Are you okay? "His eyes didn't shift from hers, as he held her in his arms.

"Yes," she mumbled, through the cape. She wanted desperately to reach out to him, to touch his face, to kiss those lips so dangerously close to her mouth. She wanted the safety and protection that kissing him promised. But she wasn't sure he'd want that and she didn't want to risk rejection.

"I'm fine," she said, wriggling a little as her face burned. Her heart hammered as his eyes comb over her body.

"You can put me down now. I must weigh a tonne," she said. It felt so good being so close to him she didn't want him to let her go.

He lowered his arms and placed her upon the antique rugs

spread across the floor of the royal tent. "You'll be perfectly safe," he said reading her apprehension. "We just have to wait it out."

She was acutely aware of every tiny movement his fingers made, aware of the brush of his skin against hers, as he unwound her cape and stared into her panic-stricken eyes.

She stepped back, her body aching with need as he drew her closer.

He reached for her hand and held it in his reassuring palm as he led her away from the entrance toward the bed.

"I could have lost you. I could not have lived with myself," he rasped. "You were mesmerising tonight," he said, his tone softening. His golden eyes blazed with fire. The hungry need she saw etched in his face stunned and stirred the smouldering desire within her.

The sandstorm barrelled upon them casting the moonlight from the tent. "Would you like me to light the candles?"

"Please," she said. The desire to see all of him eclipsing her fear as he lit the long-tapered beeswax candles mounted in the gold candelabras. A sweet honeyed scent infused the air. She felt lightheaded, weightless, and dizzy.

He advanced toward her and cupped her face in his hands. He lowered his head to hers. His firm lips seared her mouth with his hot urgency, his kiss sure and confident.

She was barely aware of the sandstorm gathering in fury, raining in rage, as an explosion of sensation blazed through her.

Her mind went blank. Emptied of everything but the promise of him as Tariq's tongue danced with hers in a seductive waltz. She felt the skilled, confident slide of his fingers down her spine, them his deft fingers unravel the fabric bow of her sequinned brassiere. His hands quickly shifted to cup her breasts as they fell into his waiting palms, sending shock waves of pleasure surging through her.

He raised his lips to her nipples and kissed them again and again, parting her flaming red skirt with his free hand.

Releasing her, he wrenched his long white robe over his head. His muscular chest glistened with sweat, and the flickering candlelight washed him in a golden glow.

She stared at the dark march of coarse black hair that ran from the centre of his chest, then disappeared below the waist of his tight-trunks. Her body pulsed with aching need.

She felt his eyes upon her as he waited with the still, powerful poise of a man aware of the sheer magnetism he wielded.

He drew a ragged gasp as she ran her fingers beneath the elastic of his underwear and felt the rising swell of his arousal as she freed him.

She wanted to slow everything down. She wanted an antidote to the wild, furious sandstorm lashing the tent outside.

She took the impressive thickness of him in her palm and cradled the most intimate part of him. Her hands glided down the length of his shaft. As her hand slid against the most private part of him excitement and longing welled in her.

Tariq's eyes glittered as he wrenched her hands-free and pulled her into him, taking her mouth in a hot burning kiss as he lifted her back against him. Ridding himself of his *keffiyeh*, the traditional square cotton scarf, he held in place with a strong black cord, he tossed them to the floor and lowered himself upon her his weight pressing her into the softness of the luxury sheets.

He slid his leg along her thigh so that she felt the roughness of his skin against the smoothness of hers. She gazed into his beautifully rugged face; her body ached with hunger.

CHAPTER FORTY-ONE

"I want to go slow," she rasped. "I don't want this night to end." She slid her palm over the firm contours of his broad shoulders, surprised by the tension she felt. He was struggling to hold back. Struggling to take his time. Struggling against a powerful urge to claim her.

Then he kissed her again, as though he knew only too well that the caress of his tongue against hers would render her powerless and drive all thoughts of languid control from her rational mind.

He played with her and kissed her with slow deliberate accomplishment. She kept her eyes open, wanting to be fully conscious, fully awake, fully aware of the longing in his eyes, and the flare of desire as he looked at her.

The raw hunger she saw she knew was mirrored in her eyes. She needed to see him. She needed him to truly see her.

"It's my role to give you pleasure, *habibti*." The endearment flowed from him so easily, as though he wasn't aware, as all his focus locked on her.

He cupped his hand over the most private part of her, making her pulse sprint. Trembling with longing, she felt the gentle slide of skilled male fingers against the mound of her moist, sensitive flesh. She felt the rhythmic circling of his touch as he traced her womanhood with slow, sensual, deliberate movements.

Tariq shifted his body, lowering it until his face was between her legs. The next thing she felt was the flaming heat of his probing tongue. Fireworks exploded in her body, as she felt his tongue on her, then enter her, exploring her in the most intimate way possible.

He drew a breath as though inhaling her scent, tasting her nectar, knowing her in every way possible until she was powerless to control her body from writhing against the silk sheets.

Only his hands pinning her wrists above her head kept her still. Skilfully he brought her to a climax, orgasming again and again, so weakened by pleasure, she could no longer resist him, merging as one, lost in time, lost in space, lost to her old way of being.

She gave a growl of ecstasy, arching her body, as every part of her spasmed. She felt his eyes on her she rasped, "I need to have you." She, who never allowed herself to need anyone, was now confessing her vulnerability.

A dangerous glint shone in his eyes as his mouth curved in a smile. "You commanded me to go slow. It is my pleasure to obey."

"Don't tease me, Tariq, please don't tease me. I need you. Now. I really, really need you. I need you inside me. I need all of you."

She gazed into his eyes, so hungry for him, every part of her body ached. She arched her back and she wrapped her hands around his shoulders. She slid her palm over the hard, smooth swell of his back muscles and pulled her to him.

He looked at her and she gasped. It was the first time he

had really seen her, she realised. Spread, exposed and vulnerable there was no place to hide and she realised with a start that she was the one woman to see the man behind the sheikh.

His tone was rough and raw as he mounted her. "I'm yours."

She clenched the hot, hard, thickness of him he entered her. In that moment all the pain, all the anger, all the hurt was lost to the desert storm.

* * *

Dawn rose in a wash of flaming tangerine over the shimmering desert. In the distance she saw the outline of trees and tents clustered around the small oasis Tariq had told her was one of his favourite places on earth. And she could feel why. Rather than destroy the beauty surrounding the kingdom the furious winds in the night had etched delicate furrows along newly contoured dunes.

She returned to bed and snuggled against him. The intensity of her feelings disturbed her as much as the realisation that he was nothing like she'd imagined him to be. Away from the palace, when people spoke his name their affection was not trained by duty or power or privilege but genuine admiration for the man he truly was.

She'd judged him wrongly. Someone pampered and privileged. Someone spoiled and entitled. Someone selfish and unfeeling.

Now, she realised with a mix of fear and awe, her view was like a mirage. She no longer knew with any true conviction what was real or what was an illusion.

But what couldn't be denied was the truth that he had saved her life and the depth of what was etched forever in her heart. Her chest tightened as it always did when he was near. Not the constriction that warned of impending doom, but the fragile flight against having opened her heart to him and the dangerous risk that he would abandon her again.

Perhaps she shouldn't have slept with him, but it felt so right. And what choice did she have when every cell in her body, every neuron in her mind, every valve in her heart, had screamed 'yes'.

It wasn't the fear of dying in a desert storm that frightened her most, it was the fear of never making love to him again. And the death of the hope that perhaps one day her dream might come true and they would live as a happy, loving family.

"*Sheikha,*" the softness of his voice as he stirred against her sent quivers trailing down her spine." How long have you been awake?"

"Long enough to know you were right, this is the most beautiful place on earth. Even the wildest of storms yield their own surprises," she said, kissing him. "I only hope my designs do it justice."

CHAPTER FORTY-TWO

The months had sped past and her creativity had blossomed. Melanie's heart gave an exultant leap as she stood back and surveyed the presentation one last time. "Finished at last!"

Then, like a fast-moving sandstorm, gritty panic ripped through her chest. She was always anxious before a presentation but never like this. Never to the point where she felt like vomiting. She placed her hand on her belly and took a deep breath.

"He'll love it," she said, noticing the heaviness in her gut that told her she was deluded. "He'll be delighted," she affirmed, noticing the clutch to her heart. "Elated," she told herself, noticing the shallowness of her breathing. None of her attempts at self-soothing had the desired effect. The truth was she was petrified.

She glanced over at her concepts and the drawings, models, and paintings she had prepared that showed the buildings as if seen from a helicopter. As always she had over-prepared. She knew from experience that she could not afford to leave anything to chance. But why was she so nervous? What was different?

*She wanted to please Tar*iq.

Unlike other commissions Tariq had believed in her, encouraged her, and gone out on a limb to champion her design. And now she had the most crippling feeling she would be a disappointment. She wasn't good enough.

What if he found out she had no talent? Or worse—what if his reaction proved her critics right? That she, the maverick, the outsider, had no place in the hallowed halls of architecture.

She was risking it all. She was risking her chance to be loved. When she showed Tariq her design she would destroy her dream. She wouldn't be able to lie to herself anymore. She would have to concede defeat. Give up architecture. Give up love. She would have nothing.

What had she been thinking? She should never have accepted his offer. Fear drummed through her heart as she heard Tariq's footsteps along the marbled corridor and the familiar authoritative sound of his voice as he dismissed his servant.

Melanie glanced at the imposing engraved double doors and imagined hurling herself against them, barricading her and her designs from capture. She would keep her dream in her own secret world.

But the thought came too late.

Tariq's imposing figure paused in the doorway. His eyes fixed on the designs behind her. His brow furrowed, as though grappling with the force, puzzling over the complexities of her work.

His silence was excruciating—far worse than any attack her critics had wielded upon her before. Her inability to read him was jarring. Why didn't he just come right out and say he hated it?

She braced herself for what he would say, she had heard it all before— her design was polarising, a magnet for controversy. She imagined her retort. 'My design is based on a simple philosophy—the meaning and power of architecture lie in its forms; the more striking and unorthodox the better. I'm not Angelina Jolie running around saving the planet. It is not architecture's job to save the world—nor your kingdom. That, Your Highness, is your job.'

He started speaking. His words slow and purposeful, his tone, grave, somber and formidable. "Radical, fantasy, theatrical. Everything shiny and new." His face was impassive, giving nothing away.

"You hate it."

He stood in front of one of the sketches, studying it with the same reverence that people view paintings in a prestigious gallery. "These are works of art," he said.

"Is that a compliment?" She said, aware of the confusion weighing her words with uncertainty.

"It is."

Was he playing with her? "I like drawing," she said, her confidence reassured.

"So I can see."

"It takes a long time to master drawings. But the digital world has taken it away. Many people can't hand render anything anymore. It's a dramatic change."

"You have gone to great lengths to make your concept tangible. I like that," he said.

Her heart skipped. Another compliment. This time, instead of swatting his appreciation away, she allowed his words to alight upon her like a butterfly. He was business-like and the consummate CEO of propriety. She appreciated that he didn't demean her with sexual references or merge the private intimacies they had shared and devalue her professional skill with verbal foreplay. Rather than unsettle her, it only made her love him more.

No respect. No love. Simple.

He walked to the table and studied the cardboard model she had crafted. He circled the table taking it in from every angle, then turned slowly toward her. His lips were pressed in a firm line as though wondering how to break the news.

Suddenly her confidence drained, and she was propelled back to the familiar feelings she had as a child when her mother complimented her on the one-hand then whacked her across the head with a back-handed criticism.

"You told me not to reign in my imagination, you knew that about me. You told me that nothing was off-limits to me. There were no boundaries," she said, defiantly.

She would not budge. She would not yield. She would not allow her designs to be belittled. She would fight for her dreams.

"So I see," Tariq said. "As always you have taken things to extremes."

"I don't like the word compromise. I never promised to be dull."

His eyebrows arched. "No. You didn't. Tell me, what was the inspiration behind your design?"

She decided to muzzle her retort. She wanted to say, 'I prefer my buildings to do the talking. Architecture, good architecture should speak to your soul.'

But his question was a fair one. Every artist should be prepared to defend their vision. She had to remember he was bankrolling the project and it was not unreasonable to want to understand it. Even though he was the all-powerful leader of Avana, Melanie knew Tariq believed in democracy. He would want his people to be excited, not divided, by her design. To help him achieve that she needed to spell out to him the clarity behind her abstract design.

And so she began to tell him how all her talks with the people she had met since coming to Avana, all the animals she had seen, and the beauty of the landscape—how all these things, even belly dancing, had inspired her.

She didn't confess that the biggest sources of inspiration had been wanting to create something Tariq and Salim would be proud to say she had designed. She wanted to keep that in her heart until the building was actually a reality.

CHAPTER FORTY-THREE

"Our ancient ancestors believed that every place has a spirit looking after it or embodying it: just as you have a soul, the land too has a soul," Tariq said, looking directly at her.

"The soul is our essence. The earth, the plants, trees, birds, sea—all things God has created have their own essences. Authenticity is power—and you Melanie, have it in bucket loads."

She felt a gush of relief whoosh from her chest. Inwardly she did a merry dance, outwardly she said calmly. "I'm pleased."

"What you have created is magnificent. You have created the soul of Avana—one which will take us into the future and cement us as true leaders. We need to fix our souls. Our souls have been broken by war, and greed, and corruption. Our souls are broken in this nation. We have lost our way. And it begins with inspiration. It begins with leadership. Together we can do this, we can be this, we can unite our people—and the world."

"You like it. You really like it?" she said finally, still

disbelieving, still thinking she was living in a dream of her own creation.

“I love it. It’s astonishing. It’s ground-breaking. It’s earth-shattering. You have smashed architecture’s glass ceiling.”

"Really?” Was he being honest? Hadn't she heard the platitudes before? From men, governments, people with the power to make or break a career. Men who overtly said they loved her designs, that they had chosen her above all else, and then broke their promises and never built them.

She frowned. Was he trying to let her down gently? Was he cheerleading her design to her face and then behind her back steadfastly refuse to build it. Ghosting on her like other design committees had. But Tariq was the design committee and he was saying all the right things.

“Why can’t you believe me?” Tariq asked.

“I’m trying. But it’s like I have gremlins in my brain, and they keep shaking up the past.”

“What do you mean?”

“I’ve heard it all before. The last time nearly killed me. It was so dire. I looked fine, but beneath it all, it was such a depressing time,” she bit her lip, wondering if she really wanted to go there. “I was practically ghosted. Publicly I was humiliated. The Prime Minister went on television and said, ‘this project is canceled.’ No one called me,” she smiled weakly trying to show she was kind of over it.

“I tried to call, I tried to talk I even flew to Japan. But there was a blank. I could be sued for saying this, so I’m trusting you with this confidence, but it was clear they didn’t want a foreigner to create a national building in Japan. On one level, I get patriotism. On another, it’s so confining. Countries don’t have a monopoly on talent. So when you opened up the possibility to me, of course, I was dubious. I have good reason to be. There's some pretty amazing talent in the East. But, yeah, it was shocking."

"I can assure you I am a promise keeper. You have my word."

She studied her sandals. Hadn't Tariq done the same thing when he'd ghosted her? Ghosts don't tell people they are getting married. Real men do. "I hope so. I really hope so," she said, deciding not to pick over the scabs of the past.

"Because when I build it and I assure you I will, I want you to be happy more than I want to break tradition. You deserve the accolades this design will bring. It's worthy of an award."

She shrugged. "Let's just get it built."

"It will be built," he reinforced. "Avana desperately needs to evolve, and this building will achieve that. I want to modernise how women are treated as well. Appointing you and ensuring your design is not just a paper-building but is actually built will shout to the world that I am not just talk. That my mission to create equality is real. Your design is sheer brilliance. The understated elegance masking a hidden strength. It stands out—unlike other museums. It doesn't cower. I like that in a woman. I love it in you."

CHAPTER FORTY-FOUR

In that moment, even though her fearful mind was yelling heartbreaker, she wanted desperately to know that whatever happened in the future his love and admiration was unconditional.

"Your design is singularly beautiful," he said. "Again, like you."

"The design emerged," she said, noting the strident march of confidence in her voice. "I didn't try to make it stand out, nor did I wish it to blend in. It's very contextual. Every little line related to an energetic point in the landscape, using the existing geometries of the terrain, rather than mimicking. It's layered, like archaeology. It came from that side."

As she spoke, she heard the rationality of it all. That cerebral side of herself conveying little of the depth of her emotions.

"I wanted to create a profound sense of belonging—to the place, to the people. To the future that lies in wait. And you'll notice that floral motifs abound just as they do in Islamic Art. As you know they are often associated with ideas of paradise, wellbeing, and other blessings. I knew this was important to you and to the success of the sanctuary."

She swept her hand over the undulating curves of the model, following the rhythm of the geometric forms. If you look closely, you'll see the roof line follows those of the petals of an orchid. The most highly coveted of ornamental plants. The delicate, exotic and graceful orchid represents love, luxury, beauty, and strength," she said.

"In ancient Greece, orchids were associated with virility," she said. "I thought, as the sponsor, the theme suited you perfectly. The word 'orchid' is derived from the Greek word *orchis* which means testicles." She hurried over the definition, anxious to ensure her intent was not to evoke desire but to provide clarity to the symbolic meaning.

"The name originates from the shape of the root tubers of the plant. It is due to this reason that orchids have been associated with sexuality in many cultures. Plus, unlike most flowers that have round-shaped petals, orchids have petals in geometrical shapes. Because of their symmetry, and the straight lines on their petals, orchids represent beauty in symmetry, and are considered epitomes of rare beauty."

"Beauty and virility. How beautifully conceived," his eyes glittered. Of course, we want the animals that find sanctuary here to flourish and reproduce."

"Of course," she said, hoping he didn't notice the sexy friskiness that lifted her voice. "Then there is love," she continued. "Orchids are considered symbols of love because of the fact that the plants grow easily, and bloom under most conditions."

"Even when things seem barren?" he asked.

"Yes, even in the most inhospitable climates. Even when they are neglected, they still show love. Her thoughts momentarily floated to the way she had blossomed since coming to Avana, despite the struggles they had faced—and still faced.

"During the Victorian era, it was a custom to gift exotic and rare flowers to show love and affection," Tariq said, suddenly choosing to reveal his supreme knowledge of botany.

"It was even believed that the rarer the flower you chose as a gift, the deeper was your love. In parts of Europe, orchids were seen used as a key ingredient in love potions. You, Melanie Jones, have given me the perfect gift—the rarest of orchids—a building of sublime beauty and unparalleled elegance. I am indebted to you."

She should have been thrilled by the compliment, were it not for the little tuber, the little symbol of their love that had yet to flower in the fullness of truth. She would tell him that night, she decided. Hopefully Tariq was in the mood for celebrating.

She had thrown everything at the project, unleashed her most innovative, visionary, futuristic designs. She had taken the most rebellious part of herself, drawn upon all the worst of the criticisms her detractors had thrown at her.

Impractical. Bossy. Brazen. She abandoned their hold over her and put her critics to the test. In doing so she had sought to free herself of her belief that to be accepted she had to remain passive, servile, small, and—heaven forbid—even nice.

She gave all that up and risked it all. Because in the end, she knew all that mattered, all that would remain, all that would be validated was *love*.

Love of her design. Love of her work. Love of her soul. Maybe, even love of her as a woman. And, if tonight went well, love for her as Tariq's son's mother.

And in that moment, she cried tears inside. Not tears of

sadness, or victory. But something deeper. Finally, she felt free. She recognised she no longer had to accept other people's authority over her, nor other people's visions for her life.

But she told Tariq none of that. Instead, she merely said, “Thank you.” Even those words, those two little words were huge in magnitude.

But she knew if she was to truly free herself of the past she must give. She must offer him something of herself. And so, she offered the only thing she could—a glimmer of her vulnerability.

“Thank you for believing in me. Thank you for allowing me to be free to be me.”

Melanie’s heart felt as if it were trying to escape from her chest as she prepared to say the words she had longed to tell Tariq for three long and lonely years.

“I have another creation I would like to gift you tonight—if you will have it.”

CHAPTER FORTY-FIVE

Hamad knocked on the door to Tariq's study and waited for Tariq to grant him entry.

"Zayed cannot return. You know that as well as I. It is forbidden. He abandoned his country," Hamad said, as he moved quickly across the room.

Tariq didn't look up from the documents he was signing, sealing the protection of three more orphaned giraffes. He was anxious to get dressed for dinner and looking forward to receiving the gift Melanie had promised. What could she possibly give him that she hadn't already?

"You oversaw the application agreement. He may never return alive or dead." The implied accusation caused Tariq's gaze to rise sharply, pinning Hamad beneath his contemptuous glare.

"Yes I oversaw it," he bit, tired of Hamad's continual disruptive attempts to undermine his decisions. "And yes he abandoned his duty. But he didn't do it because he didn't love us. He did it because we refused to love the woman he loved. He was a man, a mortal, a lover—not a saint. And it's time the people of Avana looked into their own hearts and sought forgiveness for the prejudices we all displayed. We're all guilty. You as much as I."

Hamad remained stoic and resolute. "Forgiveness," he said, "you speak of it so freely, cousin. It's easy to forgive the dead. But can you forgive the living?"

The raw, poisonous edge to his tone zigged-zagged up Tariq's spine. "What is it you want, Hamad? Beside my crown?"

"Believe me I take no pleasure in this, but if it were me, I would want to know." His voice was sweet as honey but stickier than treacle. He slid the embossed envelope across Tariq's desk with feigned remorse.

The envelope was wrapped in a thin gold string and Tariq recognised Zayed's family seal. "As you instructed I made preparations for Zayed's return. I anticipated your decision. I didn't anticipate what I found."

Tariq's wary eyes grazed the parchment lying on the table between them.

"Documents that change everything."

"What sort of documents?"

"You'll find all the answers you seek there," he said, forcing his finger to the paper. "Words spoken can lie. Written words say what cannot, or *will not*, be spoken," he stepped back from the table to leave Tariq to his own discovery.

As he reached the doorway, he turned, his imposing frame filling the space. "Sometimes, forgiveness is too high a price to pay."

CHAPTER FORTY-SIX

"When were you going to tell me?" Tariq thundered, as he stormed into Melanie's studio.

Melanie looked up from her computer as he flung the court forms across the room. She recognised them immediately. Her gaze darted to her signature. That fateful heart-wrenching signature that had sealed all their fates. Until it hadn't.

"I tried....that night— she stammered. "I tried to tell you."

"You should have tried harder." His shoulders were rigid with tension and rage.

"It wasn't meant to be like this. I wanted to tell you. I just wanted to do it properly. I was going to tell you tonight."

"Properly? Excuse me if I am unfamiliar with the etiquette book on how to tell someone you profess to love, that you have concealed the truth about their love child. That you have concealed the truth about your lover's own blood-line. That you have concealed the truth for over three damned years," he thundered.

"And worse right under his very nose you have continued the deception. Allowing the man you say you love to believe that his own son belongs to his dead brother. How the hell do you do that properly?"

Melanie sat stunned, disbelieving, hating herself for causing him so much pain.

"You must take me for a fool. There I was blindly thinking you were hiding a delicious gift—that you wanted to surprise me—and all the while you were hiding *my child.*"

"Tariq, I can explain," she slid off the chair and went to him. She tried to wrap her arms around him, unable to bear the pain and the hurt she had inflicted. It went beyond what she had imagined. She didn't know what she imagined. How could she?

He shook his head and stepped beyond her reach. "You must think I'm a monster."

"No, I don't."

"A heinous villain."

"No, I don't. No."

"A ruthless despot. You must think all of those things are true. Why else would you hide my son?"

"I didn't. I don't. No. No. No!" she cried, "I thought none of those things. Why won't you let me hold you? Why won't you let me comfort you? Why won't you let me tell you the truth?"

"What and feed me more lies?" he clasped his head in his hands. "You got me good. You'd think I'd learn. Did you think I would never discover the truth? Are you deluded? I don't even know who you are. What you are," he spat.

"The truth always prevails—eventually. I can't even begin to describe how I feel. But wait, it gets better. Do you know what the worst of it is? I'm the ogre who has to tell my son.

Do you hear me? *My Son*. The mother he thought was his mother isn't his mother. That his real mother, the mother he thought was dead, as actually alive—only she's leaving."

"I'm not leaving."

"No, you're not. You've already left. Now go. Go before you infect us with your lies. After all this time, after all these days—after everything I've done for you. After I gave my heart to you. I thought it hurt when my grandfather was murdered. I thought it hurt when my cheating, wife died. I thought it hurt when my mother left. But it turns out they were just scratches. What really hurts is to be lied to by the woman you really love. *Loved,*" he corrected.

"Is this what you came for? Retribution? Revenge? Retaliation? Because my father *made me* marry another woman?"

"You're angry."

"No," he said, his fury subsiding. "I'm absolutely heartbroken. I'm devastated that you thought so little of me. Do you have any idea what this feels like?" he said, turning from her. "Don't bother answering, I can't believe a thing you say."

"Have you finished your monologue?" Melanie said. "I'm not your punching bag. I don't have to listen to your tirade. You haven't given me a chance to say how sorry I am. And I am. I truly am. I wish I could rip the pages from the calendar. I wish I could change what happened. I wish—Tariq I wish you would look at me. I wish, God I wish more than anything that you'd give me a chance to explain before you banish me from your life."

He shook his head and remained with his back to her.

"Fine, toss me out, Mr. Promise-keeper. But where I go Salim goes."

"Over my dead body," he said, spinning around. His eyes met hers, pinning her with the full force of his fury.

"Don't even say that. Don't even joke about that," she said, wiping the tears as they blurred her vision.

He rammed his body into the plump chair by the window, thrust his legs wide and flung his arms over his chest, locking them into position high above his heart.

"Go on then. enlighten me."

CHAPTER FORTY-SEVEN

"I had to work my ass off to get noticed in this male-dominated, infuriatingly conservative career. But what would you understand?" she flew at him. "You were born with a silver spoon in your manicured hand and 1001 royal camels to ferry your royal butt around. What would you know about poverty, or trying to build a career under your own efforts? Not because it's been handed to you, or because you're the ruling class. What would you know? You're a male"

She was grasping, trying to find some way of redeeming herself. The truth was she was beyond redemption. She hated what she had done. Hated that she hadn't been strong enough. Hated that she wasn't wondrous enough to have it all. A husband, baby ,and career.

And she hated that she'd been too proud to ask him for help. But pride wasn't something she wanted to hang onto anymore. She wanted him to see her. *The real her.* The conflicted, messed up, guilty, flawed woman who knew she had to atone for her mistake.

"There wasn't a day when I didn't wonder if I made an

error, that I didn't wonder whether I should have sacrificed my career, got a job at Walmart, made coffee or swept floors. But you know as well as I do, our child deserves better than that. He is the son of a prince, a king, the sheikh of sheikhs. He's not a Jones. Not a commoner. Not a pauper.

"So, I did the best I could. When my sister Charlotte confided that she'd been trying for a baby with your brother, when she cried on my shoulder after finding out she would never be a mother, well, what can I say? It was if the fates had blessed us all. It wrenched my heart to give my baby up. It almost destroyed me. If it hadn't been for work, I think I would have died. But I told myself, convinced myself that I was doing the best thing for everyone."

She glanced at Salim's playpen, and was thankful that Latifa had taken him for a treat. She didn't want him to hear his parents arguing as she had as a child.

"My baby, *our baby*," she corrected, "wasn't going to be raised by a stressed-out working single mom. Nor was he going to be raised by a mother who didn't know if one day she would resent him like my mother did. I didn't want that for him. And I didn't want to abandon him to strangers. I sacrificed my love for him to ensure he was going to be with his family. *His blood family*. My sister and your brother."

A grim line crested Tariq's lips. He stood still, giving nothing away. Impenetrable—and infuriating as always.

"I told myself that he would be loved. And he was. They loved him deeply. And they would have kept loving him deeply. But they died."

"I put my hands up—I didn't know how to tell you. I could've tried harder. I guess, I hoped that you would come to love him as a son before you knew who he really was. And I started to see that. But I couldn't bare holding onto the secret any longer. I was going to tell you tonight," she said, thrusting her hands on her hips.

"But you know what, Tariq. If you can't love me because I didn't tell you earlier, that's fine. But it will be your fault that our baby will never know the love of two parents. And it will be your fault that you will hate me for the rest of your life. I won't abide by that. You can't force me to stay. I'm not your property. I belong to me. And I won't allow my son to be raised by a recluse who hates me."

"You are not leaving," his tone was icy and unyielding.

"If you don't let me go, I'll tweet the United Nations, and Facebook Amnesty International—or whoever the damn else I can. I'll shout out to the world and tell them to come and get me the hell out of here. I might not know a lot about your royal life, but I know one thing for sure—I won't be your inconvenient, shameful, houseguest."

CHAPTER FORTY-EIGHT

"Are you sure the child is mine?" Tariq said.

Melanie was devastated. But she showed him none of it. Instead, she studied the wild orchid hanging from the tree in the courtyard.

"As a schoolgirl my initiation to the anatomy of sex was considered complete once I had finished a science class examining a flower stamen," she said.

"What do you want, money?" he gritted.

She refused to reward his accusation by looking at him and kept her gaze locked on the flower.

Then she turned to him with the full force of her indignation. No matter how furious she felt she had to concede that of course he'd wonder. Any intelligent man would. The world was full of bounty hunters, yelling claims of paternity, hoping to become well-kept wives. Stay serene, like a martial artist, not an out of control, angry person, she told herself.

"My family were ashamed of my pregnancy." She spoke slowly, hoping he didn't detect the tremble in her voice and the way her hands shook.

"I felt like I was trapped in the 1950s, not in the modern

millennium where women of all ages are unmarried mothers. I'm not saying it's a good thing. It was what it was. I didn't deliberately get pregnant if that's what you think."

"I was a fallen woman, in my father's eyes. He wanted better for me. So I did what I could and I made the ultimate sacrifice. I went to work, and I gave my son to my sister—my very married sister. I gave up my selfish need to keep my child so that my baby wouldn't suffer the stigma I did growing up with a parent who didn't want me. I knew you didn't want me."

"I never said that."

"No, your marriage to Fatima did that—very publicly. Purity. Isn't that what your parents demanded? I knew that I'd be a stain on your father's kingdom. I knew that my baby would be considered nothing. I knew they would call him the 'bastard baby.' I knew that he would always be the undesirable outsider."

"You never gave me a chance to do the honourable thing."

"I didn't have to. I knew enough from my friends' experience. I had heard enough stories of pregnant women being abandoned by men. Wives unwilling to care for their husband's love children. And then there was me—naive enough to think a future king could love me. Until he made it clear he didn't. We were all social rejects."

Tariq remained eerily quiet.

"I worked throughout my pregnancy, cleaning houses, doing people's laundry, funding my way through college, I fought hard to keep my independence. It was all I had—that and architecture. The only thing that made me feel less unworthy."

His gaze met hers. Anger and hurt were replaced by quiet understanding.

"Giving up my baby haunted me. You have to believe that, Tariq. I never held him in my arms. We had so little time together. He was so beautiful— I couldn't stop staring at him. He had perfectly defined eyebrows—not a brutal arch like mine, but a sensuous curve just like yours."

She clutched at the adoption papers on her desk.

"I tried to take a mental photograph of my child. And when I woke the morning after his birth, he was gone."

"Your sister always was a selfish woman," Tariq said. "How could she be so mean? Sneaking in and taking the child who was yours. Who was mine."

"No, it wasn't like that. I asked…no I pleaded with my sister to please just take him before my heart broke and I changed my mind. I was so afraid that I wouldn't find the strength. I was terrified that in a moment of weakness that I wouldn't be able to go through with my decision and my son's life would be forever ruined."

She swept the papers to one side and gazed out the window. "I wondered if I could pick him up and run. Run from my past. Run from my fate. Run from my mistake. But I knew it would be wrong. So I signed the adoption papers."

She turned, wrapping her arms around her chest. "My arms would physically ache to hold my child. You know, like when people lose a limb and they still feel the pain. Indescribable pain. So don't you DARE say I didn't care."

"Evidently." His tone was soft.

"I moved to New York to work. It was the busiest city on earth. I needed the distraction. And I told no-one about the baby I had lost. Because I knew if I thought about him I would plummet so low into despair or go stark raving mad and that wouldn't have been fair to Charlie and Zayed. And it suited them. They didn't want to be found by your father. After Zayed abdicated he just wanted to be free. They were protective of Salim's privacy, and I honoured their wish not to reveal anything publicly about what had happened. I didn't think I was free of our agreement and my commitment to them just because they had died. I gave them my word."

Melanie wound her fingers around the chain beneath her shirt and lifted the locket. "I gave them my heart."

"That's why I kept the truth a secret all this time. I never meant to hurt you. I only meant to spare you the pain that I have lived with every, aching day. Why can't you believe me?"

CHAPTER FORTY-NINE

"I've got trust issues because people have got lying issues," Tariq said.

"I didn't deceive you and I didn't lie," Melanie said. "I was ashamed."

"So, you hid the truth?"

"Not exactly."

"What do you mean, not exactly? You stole my child."

"You're being dramatic."

"You gave him away."

"He's my son," she flew at him.

"Our son," Tariq corrected.

"No," Melanie said, summoning the force of her conviction. "You made it clear. You didn't want a child—at least, not with me."

"This changes everything."

"No, Tariq, it doesn't. Not for you. You can go ahead and keep living your life. You can marry thirty wives and have 600 children."

Tariq's formidable brows knitted together. "I don't want to marry thirty wives."

"I will never give my heart, my body, my soul to another man. I may only ever have one child, and I will always feel blessed that it is your child. But I won't be claimed by the sheikh, and nor will my son. I'm quite capable of raising Salim alone. And I will."

"If that were true then why did you give him up?"

"I told you. I didn't think I could give him the love he needed. I didn't want…." She felt her lips quiver. *Don't cry. Don't show him weakness.*

She placed her hand on her belly and took a deep breath. After all these years of bottling everything up could she finally lift the lid on the ugly truth that had cast a shadow over her life for too long? She didn't know what she wanted to do anymore. Certainly not this. To be arguing with the man she'd never stop loving over the child she'd always dreamed of keeping.

"I didn't want to fail him," she said.

"For three years you kept my son from me." His fine nostrils flared as he fought to maintain control. "I think I'd call that failure."

"I kept him from myself."

"Then we have all failed." His eyes grazed hers with resolute determination. "You leave me with no choice."

He stood rigidly, not even looking at her. "You have given birth to my heir." Everything about him was designed to repel her.

"You will marry me."

She tried to ignore the sharp blade of pain that cut a jagged line through her heart. This was not the proposal she had held in her dreams.

"And if I refuse?"

He was brutally honest. "You will never see your son again."

CHAPTER FIFTY

"I thought it was what you wanted." Tariq stood in the doorway of the guesthouse watching as Melanie thrust clothes into her suitcase.

"This will be your home," Tariq said. "We will raise our son together. You will want for nothing. You can build a life here. A career. A reputation. All that you have ever desired."

"This is *not* my home. My life is in London. Oh, my goodness Tariq. Why are you making this difficult? You don't want a difficult wife any more than I want a controlling husband."

"I will not lose my son."

"And I will not give him up. Not again. So, what? You will marry me and we will be a happy family? Is that what you believe? Our parents tried that, and how did that work out?" she threw at him.

"I don't want Salim to be a motherless boy like I was. I won't allow him the indignity and disgrace of being a bastard, so I will take you as my wife. Problem solved."

"You will *take me*?" she said, throwing a book of orchid photography in her case. "Problem solved?"

"Yes, isn't that what you say in the West? Do you *take this* woman as your lawful wedded wife?"

Melanie frowned and exhaled a breath of loud disbelief. "For an educated man, you're pretty ignorant. Wedding vows have evolved since those archaic misogynistic rites. We've evolved. Woman no longer regard themselves as a man's property. As usual, men have been slow to catch up. But, it's all semantics. No matter what words you choose, you're missing the point."

"I am?"

"Yes, contrary to what you may believe marriage is a partnership. A woman has to agree. As in, 'Do you Melanie Lenore Jones take this Sheikh, Tariq na Hassir, as your lawful wedded husband?' *And I don't.* I don't want a belligerent sheikh. I don't want a reluctant husband. And I most definitely don't want to be married to a man out of a sense of duty."

She thrust forward the picture of a giraffe family Salim had drawn. Her heart clutched as she studied the happy yellow polka-dotted daddy and mommy giraffe, standing with their pink polka-dotted son, their faces beaming with joy.

"Salim wants a family. *A happy family.* He wants, needs, deserves love—and you haven't said you love me, or him, since you found out the truth. Not once. In fact, just the opposite. You're made it clear that you despise me. My only worth to you is my ability to design a landmark building. Well. I've done that. I kept my side of the bargain. Now I'm asking you to do something for me. I'm asking you to let me leave with my son."

"I can't."

"You can and you bloody well will. I've spent years trailing and stumbling and clawing my way through sheer hard work and torturous hours, along the misguided path to self-worth, imprisoned by my fear of not living up to my father's ambition for me to be a famous architect."

Melanie flung her traditional Arabic dresses in her suitcase. "I've spent years believing my self-worth was dependent on achieving career success," Melanie continued. "So, I guess I should thank you. You've taught me that the real path to self-worth isn't how famous or good I am at my job—it's how good I am as a woman, as a person, as a parent. It's about being true to myself and opening my heart. I did that. I gave you my heart. But you never gave me yours. I told you I loved you—and you, Tariq? What did you do?"

Tariq stood mutely, stiff as a sentry, stoic and silent.

"Yes, that's right. Nothing. You will do anything to avoid experiencing loss again—even if it means losing out on true love. Even if it means denying Salim a real family. You're imprisoned by your mistrust and your refusal to love fully. As long as you cut yourself off from others, as long as you cage how you really feel, as long as you hold onto your judgmental standards of absolute perfection, you will never feel fulfilled. And you'll never be able to give me or Salim what we need. Unconditional, authentic love."

"So no, Tariq. I won't take you as my lawfully wedded husband. And I won't be your obedient wife."

"Have you finished?" he said. "I came to tell you, I was wrong," he walked toward her. 'This whole confounded situation is wrong," his tone was low, his emotions guarded as he studied her face for her reaction. "If it wasn't for my father, none of this would have happened. We would have been together. I forgive you. I've behaved like a child. Can you find it in your heart to forgive me?"

She couldn't breathe. She couldn't focus. She couldn't

concentrate on what he just said because she wanted to run away from him, and she wanted to run into his arms at the same time. But she still hadn't heard the three little words that would confirm the grand truth.

CHAPTER FIFTY-ONE

"My brother abdicated. He threw our country into chaos. Love did that to him. Entrusting his heart did that to him. *Your sister did that to him*. You can't just expect me to open my heart again after all that happened, and say, 'dish me up the same fate.' Trust takes time. Learning to love again, takes time. You can't demand I tell you I love you."

"I thought you forgave me."

"I did. I just think it's better if we keep our hearts cold. I need to rule without distraction, without interference."

'You think I will interfere?"

"Charlotte did."

"I'm not my sister. I'm not asking you to choose. I'm asking you to love me. Unconditionally. As I am. We can do this together. True love wins. It always wins."

"You make it sound easy."

"It's not. Being in a committed, loving relationship takes work. It takes courage, bravery, a willingness to be vulnerable. Every moment I'm with you, you teach me that. Why is it you can do that for your people, what you can do that for your animals—you can't do that for yourself? Be honest with me, Tariq—what are you really afraid of?"

"My brother threw himself into love with reckless abandon—I've always been more cautious, more restrained, perhaps it's being the second born."

"I'm not buying it."

"It's my job to save the kingdom of Avana."

"How can you save Avana if you can't save yourself? Your people are fearful, distrusting, closed to outsiders—whose behaviour do you think they reflect?"

"I saw how quickly people took advantage. I witnessed how people exploited my brother's distraction. I observed how your sister…it was very clear…"

"My sister was *not* a gold-miner. A gold-miner doesn't live in constant disapproval."

"Your sister's love killed my brother."

"Love did not kill your brother. A drunk driver killed Zayed—*and Charlie.* Don't forget I lost someone that night, too. You're not the only one who lost someone they loved. I'm not my sister Tariq. When will you finally see me for me?"

"Mommy! Daddy! Please don't shout. Please don't be angry. It's all my fault. It's all because of me. I should be dead. I should have died in the car crash. Then you wouldn't be cross."

"No. My darling that's not true," Melanie said, scooping him in her arms. Mommy and Daddy love you. We were just talking." She clenched her lips, hating that she was lying. "Sometimes people who love each other talk loudly," she added.

Salim thrust his hands over his ears and clamped down hard. "Well, I don't like it. I want you to stop."

"Go play with your giraffes, Tariq," She mouthed silently

to Tariq. She leaned over, pretending to give him a make-up kiss for the benefit of their son. "Forget about us. Pour all the love you don't have for us into Noor. Noor who doesn't speak back, who doesn't place demands on you, and will never betray you with secret babies. Go on—runaway."

Tariq did not move. He did not run. He did not budge. "My brother left me," he said, at last. "My mother left me. Everyone I love leaves."

"Oh, Tariq," she said, "finally." Her heart merged with his in their shared pain. "Failure is on the cards for everyone. No one escapes this life without pain, but it's impossible to predict, and where would we be without it? Without the study of failure to spur us to reassess and rethink, progress would be impossible. Without growing through trauma we cannot evolve."

"My brother abdicated instead of standing up to my father. He could have united to rule with his wife. He could have made your sister his equal. He could have changed the constitution and made her his queen. Avana was their kingdom to rule—they should have stood together. They should have had more tenacity and conviction. My people would have respected their courage and their conviction. They would have admired their love."

He reached his arms to Salim and embraced him tightly. "Did I ever tell you I loved you?"

Salim nodded. "Yip."

Perhaps Salim had heard his soul call out to his, willing him to live, but now he wanted there to be no doubt. "I love you. I love you. I love you," he lifted his tee-shirt and blew bubble-kisses on his belly. Salim twisted and writhed in his arms. The tension in the air evaporated in the clouds of his giggles.

"I should have supported Zayed and Charlie—both of

them," he said, turning to Melanie. "Instead, I allowed my father's poisonous beliefs to infect me."

"It's not easy to go against your upbringing. But things are different now. We have a family. We have a new generation to care for and inspire. So yes, there is no certainty that our love will prevail. And that's a good thing. If you take away uncertainty, you take away the motivation to succeed. You attract complacency," she said. "Wanting to exceed your grasp is the nature of the human condition. There's no magic to getting where we already know we can go. Architecture taught me that."

"And giraffes have taught me something too," he said, laughing as Noor, bent her neck through the window.

"Really?" she said, grinning, as Salim wriggled from her arms and went to the window. "And what life lessons have giraffes taught you?"

CHAPTER FIFTY-TWO

"Never mind how hard you fall, always remember to pick yourself up and get back on your feet," he said. "The birth of a baby giraffe is quite an earth-shaking event—literally. The baby falls from the warmth and safety of its mother's womb, high up—eight feet above the ground. The poor we thing shrivels up and lies still, too weak to move."

"Gosh, I never thought about that. It must be an awful shock being born," Melanie said.

"And confusing too. The mother giraffe lovingly lowers her neck to smooch the baby giraffe. And then just when the baby is feeling safe again, she lifts her long powerful leg and kicks the baby giraffe, sending it flying up in the air and then plummeting to the ground. As the baby lies curled up trying to recover, the mother kicks the baby again."

"I don't think I like this story," Melanie said, screwing her face. "I thought I had a mean mother."

"And then she kicks her baby again. Until the baby giraffe, still trembling and tired and frightened, pushes its limbs and for the first time learns to stand on its feet.

Delighted to see the baby can stand on its own feet, the mother giraffe gives it yet another kick—just to be sure. The baby giraffe falls one more time, but this time recovers quickly and stands up. Mommy Giraffe is thrilled," he said.

"She knows that her baby has learned an important lesson: Don't worry about how hard you fall, always remember to pick yourself up and get back on your feet."

"Why does the mother giraffe do this? Surely she can teach her baby how to stand up a different way?"

"She knows that lions and leopards and other predators love sweet giraffe meat. So unless the baby giraffe quickly learns to stand and run with the pack—it will be left for dead. It will have zero chance of survival. Most humans are not quite as lucky as baby giraffes. No one teaches us to stand up every time we fall. When we fail, when we are down, we just give up. No one kicks us out of our comfort zone to remind us that to survive and succeed, we need to learn to get back on our feet."

"I've been living in my comfort zone for too long. And it's taken you and Salim to bring me to my knees. It's taken you and our son to take me to the edge. It's taken fighting to keep you both here to teach me how to stand up in a different way."

He turned to her and kissed her. "Have I told you recently that I loved you?"

"Yip," she lied. Well it wasn't exactly a lie. He had shown his love in a thousand and three different ways. People didn't always have to say it in words, she told herself. Words can lie. But actions were where you saw the truth.

"If you study the lives of successful people though, you will see a recurring pattern," Tariq said. "Were they always successful in all they did? No. Did success come to them quickly and easily? No, no! You will find that the common streak running through their lives is their ability to stand up every time they fall. The ability of the baby giraffe! I hope, when my time on this earth ends, people will study my success and they will learn that is is the ability of a woman and a child to teach the most important life lesson of all. Love makes us stronger."

He snapped his fingers and thirty or so servants came striding in, their arms filled with bouquets of scented orchids.

"I love you. I adore you. You are my light. My love. My reason for being. You make me want to be a better man."

CHAPTER FIFTY-THREE

"What's going on?"

Tariq said, navigating the maze of 1000 count cotton sheets draped over the gilt-edged chairs in the cavernous dining room.

Melanie held a finger to her lips. "Get down, or he'll find us."

Tariq hesitated. His black eyes connected with her and sent a shock wave to her stomach.

"Come on, you'll blow our cover." Melanie threaded her fingers around the hem of his long white *dishdashi* and kept tugging until Tariq reluctantly yielded.

She wriggled her bottom back along the plush Turkish prayer rug making room for Tariq's powerful frame. He folded the length of his legs with the awkwardness of a giraffe. His knees knocked against hers as he crossed them, sending a frisson of blazing awareness through her body.

He looked at her, and she could see, that despite his air of annoyance and formality that he was clearly amused. The humour of the most powerful man in the world kneeling at her feet didn't escape her.

"I daresay tongues will wag if we are discovered," he laughed.

"I doubt your reputation would suffer. In fact, just the opposite. I think it would be good if more world leaders showed a softer, more playful side."

"I can think of more pleasurable things to do beneath bedroom sheets," he said.

"Spending time with Salim enriched my work," she said, attempting to distract him as sexual energy sparked between them. "You already have people's respect. It wouldn't harm you to show your humanness."

"Is that even a word?" he asked, concealing the barest thread of a smile.

"I found you mommy!" Salim cried, his giggle running ahead of him until he at last reached the tented chairs.

"Mommy loves daddy," he said, discovering them kissing as he threw himself to the floor and peered under the covers.

Melanie's heart skipped as the warm whoosh of his breath blew her hair across her face. Hearing him call them both and seeing the joy on his face was like ice-cream without the calories. She never thought such happiness was possible.

"Mommy and I built a fort," Salim, said plopping himself in his father's lap, "To play hide and seek."

"So I see."

As Tariq rose to his feet, the frenzied sweep of rainbow-coloured paint caught his attention. He glanced down at his son's fingers, stained with emerald, sapphire and crimson ink.

"You allowed him to do this?" he said, as he took Melanie's hand and pulled her to her feet.

"He has talent. It's very Jason Pollock, don't you think?" she said, glancing over at the wall once painted stark white and now a riot of squalls, splashes, and whimsically etched letters of the alphabet.

Tariq snapped his fingers to summon his servants. Salim wriggled out the tent and stood by his father his spine straight as a new pencil. He stared into Tariq's appalled face and began to cry.

Melanie watched, wondering how Tariq would react to what surely he would regard as weakness. Boys don't cry. Sheikhs don't display emotion. Future kings don't lose the plot over childish scribbles.

But instead of scolding Salim, and telling him to toughen up, Tariq lifted him up and cradled him pressing him against his chest. He held him momentarily and then set him down.

"Leave us," he commanded his servants. "Did you like my joke, son?" he said. "I was teasing you. I'm sorry. Your mother is right. You do have talent. Lots of it. More than the moon and the sky. Do you know what I am going to do?"

Salim shook his head. He pointed to the ceiling above the painted wall. "I am going to have museum lights there, so we can spotlight your artistic masterpiece."

Melanie's heart sauntered a happy dance. She knew what a big step this represented. Tariq, who preferred order and formality above all else, was signalling that a little crazy chaos was just perfect. And more than that. He was showing that he was capable of loving his son unconditionally. There was still a long way to go, but it was a start.

"Let's hide from mommy," Salim said, smiling as he wrapped his chubby hand around his father's fingers.

She watched as Tariq placed the boy down and slipped his hand over Salim's, closing it softly around the boy's.

For so long, she had ached for her son to know what she never did—the safety and security of two loving parents. Silently she wept.

She told herself it didn't matter that Tariq had not proposed after her first, and second refusal. She just hoped that even though they weren't married that there wouldn't come a time when they would force their son to choose.

CHAPTER FIFTY-FOUR

"Oh my god!" Latifa suddenly let out a scream, as Melanie and she sat eating breakfast.

"What?" Melanie said, anxiety rising in her chest. She was so used to disapproval, so used to bad news, she'd become used to bracing herself for the worst. Tariq had done his best to convince her that the worst was over, but he hadn't successfully persuaded her yet.

Latifa was smiling as she swiped her finger along the screen of her iPhone and scrolled through the news article. "It's an opinion piece all about this year's most inspiring architecture," she looked directly at Melanie, her smile broadening, "You'll never believe it, Lani! You've been nominated for The Ritzher prize."

Latifa read the article out loud, her voice saturated with pride and importance. "And they're picking th*at H*ABI will win the supreme prize—and Stephen Rogers has a proven track record of picking the winners," Latifa said breathlessly. "Wow! How do you feel?"

"Honestly? I don't mean to sound pessimistic, but I've been nominated so many times before and I've always been disappointed. In the 50-year history of The Ritzher a woman has never won. I don't play golf, and I don't smooze, and I'm not rubbing the egos or lining the pockets of the men who choose the winners. So, I've learned not to get my hopes up. It's nice to have the attention but at the end of the day whether I win or lose doesn't really matter." Melanie forced a smile, fully aware she was lying to herself to avoid disappointment.

"What matters is that I've created the building I wanted to design, I haven't lowered my vision to meet someone else's expectation of what good architecture is—or isn't."

"It's still nice to win a prize," Latifa said. "If you keep expecting to be disappointed that's what you're going to get back. Try and cultivate more optimism. See yourself victorious."

Melanie regarded her skeptically. "Have you been listening to Tony Robbins?" she said, deciding to concede a little. "Being nominated is a great honour, and it's good for my portfolio."

Perhaps Latifa was right. Perhaps she had spent her whole life battling so much that she was sending out the wrong vibe. Not just in her design work but in her romantic life too. Would it be so reckless if she allowed herself the luxury of believing she could win—in love and in life?

She tried it on for size, turning toward the images she conjured in her mind, floating on a shimmering gold-coloured ocean she knew she wanted to swim through. She felt Tariq's embrace as her name was called, she saw the pride in his eyes as she gave her speech. She tasted the sweet, sensual bouquet of accolades as her award-winning design displayed upon the screen. She heard Tariq's deep, mesmerising voice telling her that he had always been her number one fan as they celebrated her win that evening in bed.

And for the first time, Melanie allowed herself to admit that it would be amazing to win The Ritzher prize and it would be incredible to attend the awards ceremony with Tariq by her side.

As his wife. If only he would ask her again.

Suddenly she had something to look forward to. Not just the prospect of winning the coveted prize which had eluded her all these years, but how it incredible it would feel if both her dreams could come true.

Then, as if by magic Tariq called her from Milan and congratulated her on the nomination and told her how much she deserved to win. He told her that he would fly back immediately and suggested a date night to celebrate.

Her heart was pounding. "Yes, let's!"

CHAPTER FIFTY-FIVE

"I haven't had this much fun in years," Melanie said, glancing down at they went hot air ballooning over the desert to celebrate her nomination.

"Neither have I. I can't even remember the last time I laughed so much," Tariq said. He turned to her earnestly. "Do you know how much joy you have brought into my life?"

"And you mine," she said, plopping a rich, plump date in his mouth.

"You are an incredible woman, Lani. I feel honoured to know you, honoured to have met you, honoured to have fathered a child with you. I never thought I would get over the grief of losing my brother, but now I see, his death has brought us closer together. It has made us a family. We have helped each other through some of the hardest events of our lives, and we have endured some of the most testing times. We have seen each other in sickness and in health, our fears and our flaws, our deepest failings, and vulnerabilities—and I know now what unconditional love is. I know now that I shall love you to the end of days. I know now that what we have is unbreakable. I will love you forever, in this life and those beyond."

"Oh, Tariq. I feel the same way. I love you with all my heart."

"Do you love me more than architecture?" he asked her with a cautious look.

She looked down at HABI, the museum she had designed and which was now built, in the distance. "Yes," she said softly. "I love you more than architecture. I always believed that if architecture didn't kill me, I was no good. But you've taught me that love inspires, it doesn't destroy. You have taught me that love strengthens, not weakens. You have taught me that love heals, not wounds. Your love has made me a better architect. But more than this, your love has helped me become a better woman. A better woman and a better mother. Your love has freed me."

It was time to release the past and live again. Suddenly life looked brighter. And there just might be a Ritzher Prize in her future—and a man who truly respected, and trusted and loved her.

But did he love her enough to marry her?

Melanie didn't dare pin too much hope on that for fear of jinxing everything that spoke to her heart. The future wasn't hers to predict. Winning Tariq's hand in marriage was just as speculative as the prediction her building would win The Ritzher prize.

"Would you like to go swimming?" He asked.

"Swimming? Here?"

"No, silly. Down there," he said, as the balloon began to descend.

Her breath caught in her heart. Just beyond the desert, by the edge of the turquoise sea, she could see the most beautiful, romantic, seaside picnic. Large Arabian rugs, dotted with plump cushions and a smorgasbord of delights, fit, of course, for a Sheikh.

It was almost—no. She wasn't going to get her hopes up and hope he would propose. When sheikhs and kings, and head of state proposed, they made sure everyone knew. This was all too secluded and private.

"A swim sounds brilliant," she said, hoping her voice didn't betray her disappointment.

CHAPTER FIFTY-SIX

"Isn't nature amazing?" Melanie said, as they swam in the sensual waters of the Arabian sea. Above them, the sky was awash with stars. And on the beach the fire crackled gently and filled the air with intoxicatingly spicy smoke. Tariq had thought of everything. He had packed a swimsuit with towels and a spare change of clothes, as well as arranged the most sumptuous feast.

A life of no regret. That was what she wanted. She regretted all the years she had wasted beating herself up. She regretted hanging onto fear and anger and guilt. But most of all she regretted saying, 'No. Never. No way. I won't be your wife.'

Would he ever ask her again?

His eyes glittered in the moonlight as she turned and wrapped her legs around his waist. "Do you know how freeing it is to swim bare—with nothing between you and the water? He asked.

No regrets, right? She slid the straps of her swimsuit off her shoulders, then tugged it below her breasts and down over the curve of her thighs. She felt her nipples harden. Was it the tingle of the salty sea, or the sense of exhilaration of swimming naked? She *wanted him to see her.* She wanted him to want her.

She would apply immersion therapy. She would do the thing she feared and her fear would disappear—guaranteed. She would drown those bloody regrets before they stole the future that she so badly desired. She would throw caution to the wind, or rather the water.

She would ask him to marry her.

"It's a full moon tonight in Venus. The lovers moon. And a blue moon too," she said.

"Perfect," Tariq said, "Everything couldn't be more perfect. You couldn't be more perfect," he took her hand and led her from the sea toward the fire he had built on the beach.

"Once in a blue moon the earth sends forth a coloured diamond. Intense and intriguing the stone might be yellow, pink, orange, or violet—more brilliant than the brightest star," Tariq said.

"A blue diamond? Wow, I never knew it was possible," she said, gazing up at the sky sprinkled with glittering lights. She kicked the sand gently, kicking away her self-consciousness as they stood naked before each other. She sucked in a gulp of air. Okay, she would plunge in and pop the question. No mucking about.

But Tariq was in a poetic mood. "It's fiery brilliance and exquisite colour, the most powerful emotional triggers in a gem, always come together with dramatic effect—like you," he said, his voice a sensuous crawl.

"Flatterer," she laughed. She cleared her throat. Okay, get on with it.

"I mean it. I've never met another woman like you, Melanie Jones. There's nothing common about you. Not in the least. You're rarer than that Fancy Deep Blue 20 carat diamond found in Botswana."

"There certainly nothing common about the handsome Sheikh standing butt-naked before me either," she laughed, nervously. But it wasn't the sheer beauty of his virile masculinity that made her senses zing like stars. It was the nervous anticipation of what might actually be coming next.

Was Tariq going to propose? Her body began to shake. Tiny embers of firelight drifted along the beach like tiny fairy lights.

"There is one blue diamond for every 10,000 gem-quality white diamonds found," Tariq continued, his tone suddenly earnest.

The day began just like many others and had now faded into night and they had decided to end the day with a swim. Perhaps that was it.

Perhaps he was telling her about a new investment is a diamond mine.

Perhaps, she'd missed her chance. Her brave idea of asking him to marry her drowned in a puddle of doubt.

She went to get their towels, then turned around and almost ran straight over the top of him; he was down on one knee about to propose.

She cupped her hands over her lips and clamped back an audible squeal.

Tariq reached into the picnic basket and withdrew a tiny silk purse woven from gold silk. He withdrew his closed fist and then scattered a carpet of thousands of white pearls and diamonds at her feet.

The rich orange fingers of the moon merged with the fire-light and shone on the jewels embossing their aura with extra rich intensity.

Melanie held her breath as he reached back into the hamper and withdrew a tiny velvet lidded box.

CHAPTER FIFTY-SEVEN

"Among these coveted stones, the blue diamond is considered the rarest, most captivating and most enigmatic treasure. A treasure that transpires all of time, enchanting in all its complexity—that diamond is you. Glistening in the distance as dusk casts over the flame-coloured dunes, amidst a mirage of memories, you appeared. And now I cannot imagine my life without you. Melanie Jones, will you do me the honour of being my desert queen?"

A whoosh of air shot from her chest as Tariq opened the lid and raised it to her. She gazed down at the most incredible blue diamond ring. She felt her eyes sting with tears. "Oh, Tariq."

"I'm renaming it the Jubilant Jones Diamond—on account of how you look right now—and how much joy you've brought into my life. From the first moment I saw you, it was clear I had something, a very special once-in-life-time find. A find as rare as a star in the Milky Way."

Melanie started to cry. "Tariq. My darling Tariq. I would love to be your queen—here in the desert and wherever you are." Tears streamed like rivers and plopped on the hot sand. "Yes! Yes!Yes!" she cried, pulling him to his feet.

He cupped his hands under her buttocks and lifted her high in the air and kissed her.

"This is forever, right?" she murmured.

"I didn't think I'd have to negotiate. Silly woman. Of course, this is forever, 'til death do us part and meet again in the heavens."

"And I can still be a disobedient wife?"

"I won't settle for anything less," he said.

She realised then that she was suspended in time and space, simply letting herself be carried on the tide of his love and the waves of undeniable desire she wanted to bathe in.

"Claim me," she said, kissing him over and over again under the infinite sky. "Claim me, my sheikh."

They lay down on a bed of soft, warm sand. Tariq's hands curled over Melanie's bare shoulders as his mouth slid to her neck, softly biting and suckling her sensitive skin as she trailed her fingers through his hair. She could hardly believe she was caressing the man who would soon be her husband.

He gazed at her with a love so consuming the beach suddenly seemed too large, the night too short, the days too few.

"Make love to me, Tariq."

The words were barely formed on her lips when he drew her toward him and kissed her again. This time as his mouth touched hers, he kissed her with such feeling, such warmth, such tenderness that all her fears disappeared. She folded into the softness of his lips, both of them no longer holding back the fullness of their hearts.

CHAPTER FIFTY-EIGHT

"You won!" Tariq said, turning to Melanie as they sat in the auditorium. He clutched her hand and squeezed. Not enough to bruise her, but enough to break her trance. "You won The Ritzher prize."

She'd been holding her breath, frozen between longing and feigned nonchalance. Of course she wanted to win. The problem was she didn't want to lose either. And so it was that she completely missed the announcement.

"Melanie Jones is a role model in a field that has few others," the announcer said. "That is not to say that there are not a great many accomplished and inspiring women in architecture. But none have achieved Jones's prominence—as, indeed, have few male architects."

"Against all odds and a great deal of prejudice, she broke one glass rooftop after another, no mean feat when that glass was as hard and thick and unyielding as concrete. She's tenacious, uncompromising and singularly audacious—qualities more priceless than the rarest of diamonds."

A loud round of applause quaked through the auditorium

as Melanie walked up to the podium to accept The Ritzher prize.

"I'm not going to be blasé about this," she said, grinning. Where once her traits had been regarded by her peers as her weakness they were now award-winning strengths, and she was determined to enjoy the accolades.

"It really is a great honour. It's a very special award and I would like to thank The Ritzher prize for promoting innovative architecture in this very special way. I would especially like to thank His Royal Highness Sheikh Tariq na Hassir for supporting me. And I would like to take this opportunity, for it is long overdue, to thank my father, my friends and my husband for supporting my passion for architecture. My father and Tariq encouraged my ambitions *and even my unusual obsessions*—what can I say? I am indebted to you."

Melanie scanned the audience and then turned toward Tariq and spoke directly to him. "You gave me my first platform to express my ideas—and it is you, your people and our son, Salim, who provided the inspiration. It is to you that I dedicate this award. Without you there would be no *HABI.* Without you, there would be no me."

She looked directly at him and placed her hand to her heart. "The flowering of my true potential blossomed because of you. I am here because you loved me."

He stood, looking every bit the authoritative regal ruler. And then, just when she thought she couldn't be surprised anymore, he bowed. Not the shallow bow of someone who doesn't give a toss. Not the meek bow of someone playing lip service to their deference, but the low, deep, lingering bow of a man deeply devoted.

A wave of gasps washed through the audience. The king of kings was publicly acknowledging his queen in a way no world leader ever had. Or ever would.

They stood, surrounded by people, but cocooned in silent admiration, staring into each other's eyes.Then Melanie turned to the audience. "Both these men in my life—my son and my husband—freed me from the restraint of trying to live up to others expectations. Both men loved me for being myself—and it is this love that has enabled my creativity to flourish, to blossom, to grow."

Her voice faltered, emotion overcoming her, as she recalled what Tariq had taught her. "It was Tariq who told me, 'Trust yourself. You know more than you think you do, you have a gift. You have to believe.' Tariq's faith gave me the confidence to spread my wings, and push the boundaries," she paused. "Of course his formidable wealth also helped."

The audience laughed, and she laughed with them, no longer ashamed of Tariq's money, but grateful that his wealth and his support had enabled her to do something meaningful and beneficial to the world.

"I am proud to stand here today, and accept this recognition and confirmation that the role of architecture is to erect a platform for experimentation. But it is love that provides the steel and it is love that provides the supports, and it is love that strengthens the foundations from which humanity can soar to its fullest potential."

Tariq waited for her to finish her speech and nodded his command. Thousands of orchids floated from the ceiling, bathing the audience in a fragrant mist of flowers. He joined her on the stage and kissed her. They didn't need words. They were together. They were united. They were in love. And that was all they needed. Forever.

EPILOGUE

Tariq smiled as he watched Salim interact with HABI, and he watched as the six-year-old twins ran ahead. The girls ran to their brother and turned to look back at their parents across the cavernous lobby, framed by the concrete walls and magenta accents as if they were inside a huge orchid.

It didn't matter to Salim or the twins that this was an award-winning museum designed by the first female architect to win The Ritzher prize. It didn't even matter that this spectacular, ambitious, famous building was designed by their mother.

They were instinctively and completely awed by the space itself. But as their father, as someone who hoped his children would be able to forge a career in the arts if they want to, a career over which they could have the same total freeing control as their mother, and who, through both toughness and pure virtuosity, had managed to achieve her audacious vision, it mattered to Tariq.

They were his family. His future. His destiny.

"Are you happy, Lani?" he said, as Melanie, nestled against him.

"*Ahwa.* I am in love."

"*Ahwa, habibti.*"

He smiled as he watched the little *sheikhas*, so beautiful and full of grace—and boisterously determined like their mother, run freely around the garden wall which protected the animal park within. Charlie and Zayed's bodies lay beneath a large date tree, and their souls flew free in the infinite sky. Everyone felt happy knowing they were near, nestled within the magic space of refuge and renewal Melanie had created.

And Tariq's heart roared with pride as he watched his son, the strong little lion, watch over his sisters like the protective brother he had instantly become from the day they were born. And it suddenly struck him that not only were the children growing but he had grown too.

If he hadn't broken free of his habits and weaknesses and ghosts from his past, he never would have experienced a richer and fuller life. He had become a better version of himself and in the process had created a new dynasty that would change the world.

"My heart tells me the truth," Tariq said.

"Which is?" Melanie asked.

He clutched her to his chest. "That we're all going to live happily ever after."

THE END

AUTHOR'S NOTE

This book was inspired by the sassy brilliance of Dame Zaha Hadid. (DBE RA) She was an Iraqi-British architect and the first woman to receive the Pritzker Architecture Prize, in 2004.

Tragically her life, her love, and her brilliance was cut short when she was in the prime of her career, aged 65.

Her beautiful, innovative, pioneering architecture always inspired me, as it has countless other people. Hers was not an easy journey. She once said, "If architecture doesn't kill you you're no good."

She was beyond good—and architecture did kill her. She never married and she never had children. And she was always battling the architectural paternity for validation and acceptance. Despite her career success, her life struck me as very lonely and sad.

Claimed by the Sheikh was also inspired by the tragedy in 2015 that took the lives of former New Zealand All Black legend Jerry Collins and his Canadian partner Alana Madill in France. The crash happened at 3:10 am along the highway near Béziers on the way to the city of Montpellier. They died instantly, and their baby daughter was taken to Montpellier hospital in a critical condition.

I cried such tears thinking of that baby being left an orphan. It really worried me that she would be left in the world with no parents to love and care for her.

So I wondered—what if her parents weren't really dead? What if the two people that died were the baby's adoptive parents? What if her biological parents were very much alive?

And then, as writers are want to do, I thought, what if the biological father was an extraordinarily wealthy sheikh who was unaware that he had fathered a child?

Why a Sheikh? In a previous incarnation as a transformational leadership coach I was on assignment in one the most dangerous prisons in New Zealand.

I very much admired the men and women who worked in these very oppressive environments to keep our world safe. I especially admired those that were committed to helping prisoners change their lives. One of the female prison officers at Rimutaka Prison knew that I was a romance novelist and asked me if I would write a book with a sheikh as the hero.

So here he is, Cheryl. I dedicate Melanie and Tariq's love story for you.

And I also dedicate this book to the survivors of the 2019 Christchurch mosque shootings in New Zealand—and to those around the world who know that only love can bring peace.

Read on, for an excerpt from *Stolen by The Sheikh*. Learn more about Tariq's gorgeous younger brother Anwar and the women who stole his heart.

Did you enjoy reading about Tariq's Italian friend Massimilliano Balforni, CEO of Emporio Balforni, Milan's most prestigious fashion house, and the art therapist who had induced such a miraculous, transformational change in him?

Discover more about their love story in *The Italian Billionaire's Christmas Bride*, book two in the Gemstone Billionaires series.

If you'd like to learn more about these characters, gain inside tips into the writing process, or be the first to know when a new book is released, subscribe to my newsletter here: http://eepurl.com/ghM501

Please email me and I'll be in touch personally—I promise...mollie@molliemathews.com.

THANK YOU

Thank you for reading *Claimed by The Sheikh*… I hope you loved it. If you did…

1. Help other people find this book by writing a review
2. Signup for my new releases email to find out about the next book as soon as I release it, sign up here http://eepurl.com/ghM501
3. Email me at mollie@molliemathews.com with a copy of your honest review and let me know if you'd love to join my dream team and of advance readers
4. Follow me on BookBub, https://www.bookbub.com/authors/mollie-mathews
5. Stay in touch on Facebook, https://www.facebook.com/molliemathewsnz
6. Follow me on Twitter - https://twitter.com/Molliemathewsnz
7. Be inspired on Pinterest - https://nz.pinterest.com/

molliemathews and Instagram - https://www.instagram.com/molliemathewsauthor

8. Follow my blog - https://molliemathews.wordpress.com

Keep reading for a preview of the first book in the True Love series, *Flight of Passion* and sneak peeks into other passion-filled stories including *Stolen by The Sheikh (*due for release 2020)

EXCERPT: FLIGHT OF PASSION

FLIGHT OF PASSION

BOOK ONE IN THE TRUE LOVE SERIES

AVAILABLE NOW

Past love and the obsessions that bind them.

Devastatingly handsome Oliver Hart is used to getting what he wants. Single, thirty-five and a committed bachelor, he plays by his own rules. On a personal quest to catch a rare, elusive and very valuable butterfly, he's unwittingly distracted by a former flame, Ruby Diaz—a woman who callously abandoned him eight years earlier.

Deciding he wants to reclaim the beauty as his own, in his mind, it's as good as done.

But Ruby is not his for the taking. Promised to the son of a wealthy landowner, she refuses to succumb to his charms. On a quest to save her family's land, Ruby knows she must put duty first, and silence the passionate stirrings of her heart. But Oliver doesn't make things easy for her. He's not taking no for an answer.

Risking everything to help the woman he loves to gain her freedom, Oliver entangles himself in an emotional net that alters his life forever. Sacrificing his own selfish pursuit to help Ruby, he realises that you may be able to own something, but you can never own someone—especially the women you love.

Have you ever wanted to be with someone who sent your heart soaring but threatens your sense of security? Someone who lifts you clear out of the water, but you're not sure will be around to catch you when you fall head over heels in love? Flight of Passion is a rapturous tale of beauty, obsession and the transformational power of unconditional love.

PRAISE FOR FLIGHT OF PASSION

"This is a well-written book that tantalises your senses. Will Oliver be able to convince Ruby that she loves him enough to disobey her family? Can they find each other when all seems lost? An excellent book that I highly recommend. It will have you laughing with joy and crying with sadness."

~ Marie Fraser

"Mollie Mathews has written a beautifully scripted story of two people wildly attracted to each other but too constrained by family expectations to allow themselves to commit. When they meet again after eight years can they move beyond old patterns of behaviour or are they doomed to always want, but never have?"

~ Jane Whitmeyer

"This book is a carefully crafted, truly original story. Mollie's wonderfully descriptive narrative paints a picture in which it is easy to lose oneself—I really felt like I had been to Mexico by the time I had finished. Her butterfly theme echoes throughout the book, both literally and figuratively. The main characters, Oliver and Ruby, are each conflicted in their own ways. Despite facing challenges, both ultimately find the strength to work through their difficulties to emerge better people, and most importantly, triumph over adversity together. A touching and heart-warming book, well worth a read."

~ Cathy Rioran

"Fast-paced, heart-wrenching completely unexpected twists, excellent storyline, and a hell of a good read. You just gotta love Mollie's imagination and expertise in her writing."

~ Rae Waterhouse

"I fell in love with Ruby and Oliver, they are so good for each other, but both are so filled with garbage that their families filled them with, that they can't see what's in front of them. And when they finally realise that diamonds don't have a hold to what they had, they are about to lose it. The butterflies remind me of how ethereal life is and it is up to us to not waste it, but live the fullest and best we can."

~ Advance reviewer

"I really enjoyed Flight of Passion! I loved the descriptions of the butterflies and of the setting of the farm in Mexico. Wonderfully descriptive writing that transports you to a golden orchard filled with butterflies. Perfect for a cold winter's evening curled up by the fire."

~ Linda Buckhingham

PROLOGUE

GROWING UP OLIVER WAS LEFT WITH THE impression he wasn't worthy. First by his parents who at the age of four sent him to the bottom of the world. It was as if they didn't know what to do with their infinitely curious and energetic child. It was as if sending him to the most prestigious boarding school in New Zealand absolved them of their responsibility, the responsibility which was every parents'—or should be, he thought bitterly—to love their child unconditionally.

After his run-in with a box of matches, they told him he would amount to nothing. He proved them wrong. At sixteen, he left New Zealand and headed for New York. It was true. If he could make it there, he could make it anywhere. With the ruthless determination he was both admired and feared for, like King Kong on steroids, he quickly climbed to the top of the property acquisition tree.

He was king of the beasts, the man everyone wanted at their dreary New York parties, full of chequebook philanthropists who would never stoop to get close to the people their showy donations benefitted. Parties, like the one where he'd first met Ruby Diaz

Ruby had fluttered into his life like a breath of fresh air. She had lit up the room with her illuminating presence and dazzlingly rare beauty—not just on the outside but the inside too. Her authenticity had the scent of violets—too guileless for pretence.

His darling Ruby. Oliver swallowed hard, refusing to succumb to the wave of angry hurt that swum from his heart to his throat.

For three blissful years, they were inseparable. But no matter how much success Oliver acquired, how extraordinarily wealthy he became, Oliver wasn't good enough for the Diaz's darling Ruby. He never knew why she flew from his life, disappearing as quickly as she'd arrived. She had said nothing, given him no explanation, not even the courtesy of a call.

The Diaz family and the way Ruby had callously abandoned him reminded Oliver he would never be worthy—he was unlovable. Perhaps he should thank them for sparing him further hurt. Thanks to them and his hopeless parents, he swore never to love again.

And that suited him just fine.

OBSESSION

I would like to be the air that inhabits you

~ Margaret Atwood ~

CHAPTER ONE

WOULD SELLING *BUTTERFLY LOVERS* REALLY free him of painful memories he'd rather forget?

Common sense told Oliver Hart that *Butterfly Lovers* was just a painting. An inanimate object, incapable of controlling him. But that was the trouble—it did control him, seducing him with its beauty, twisting his heart with bittersweet memories.

He'd intended to keep it . . . her . . . forever. His heartbeat seemed to almost stop as he thought of Ruby Diaz, the woman who had inspired the painting's commission. He rubbed his powerful chest, trying to ease the painful tightness that constricted his lungs as he surveyed the crowd gathered for the charity art auction.

It was time to let them both go. But would Oliver ever be free?

His gaze swept over the minimalist, exquisitely designed interior, lingering over the priceless abstract by Rothko adorning a charcoal-black wall, at Hillcrest, his newly acquired mansion, and New Jersey's most expensive country estate.

Tonight, though, it was *Butterfly Lovers* which held in its grip women dripping with diamonds, and men clad in Armani. Locked in shared awe, they clustered around the painting, studying every line, every pulsating colour.

Oliver wondered if their eyes ached as his did with a heady mix of pleasure and pain just to stand in its spell-binding presence. Or were they trying to decode the painting's hidden secrets?

Like a moth to a seductive flame, his eyes drifted to the bottom of the painting. Nobody, but one other person, would ever be able to decipher the graffiti-style line of poetry scrawled in throbbing orange along the bottom of the painting.

Painful memories bled into his consciousness. Why the hell couldn't he shake her?

Butterfly Lovers. The painting was aptly named, he mused, forcing his mind from the woman who had inspired the purchase. The dancing kaleidoscope of colour reminded Oliver of his collection of exotic butterflies—his hobbyhorse and quiet obsession.

Dazzling sapphire blues, glistening watermelon pinks, pulsating canary yellows with shimmering oranges—flew from the canvas, and ricocheted off the marble floor which had been polished to a mirror-like gleam.

He had commissioned the painting in a move of uncharacteristic impulsiveness eight years earlier when he was 22 and madly in lust with Ruby. A 20-year-old exotic beauty, she'd fluttered into his life, bringing with her eternal sunshine, and air so fresh it seeped through the iron fortress he'd built around his heart.

Butterfly Lovers encapsulated the vitality, optimism, and

positivity she exuded. It was a rare piece which the serious art connoisseurs who gathered here this evening would die to possess. Oliver's brow furrowed, aware many were drawn here not by the desire to possess the contemporary art world's finest paintings, but insatiable voyeurs hungry to glimpse the inner world of one of America's wealthiest and most elusive bachelors.

Immensely private, he'd never opened any of his palatial homes to the public before. Not homes, *houses*, he corrected. He congratulated himself as he glanced around the clinical, museum-like surroundings. The dark walls and sophisticated lighting, spotlighting priceless works of art, created a sophisticated, yet austere, facade. If a building was truly a reflection of its owner, as many designers believed, the interior aptly reinforced the stereotypes perpetuated in the media—moody, dark, mysterious and strictly hands-off.

There was some truth to that, but it was not the whole truth.

Oliver's eyes drifted to the spiralling staircase and the heavy gold braided rope barricading the entrance to the upper level. He never let anyone get beyond the ground floor of his psyche. Some tried, but few persevered. No one, other than Ruby had ever penetrated his fortified armour. And that was a mistake.

He was complicated.

No doubt someone here tonight would go home and tweet that he was something of a social outcast, and arrogant to boot, Oliver thought as he hovered in the background. The fact was that he preferred his own company than engaging with his guests—predominantly wealthy financiers and bankers.

He knew his contempt was hypocritical, given he didn't care who reached into their pockets. But there was something decidedly unpalatable about bankers and the merciless way they preyed on the vulnerable. Tonight, he would gladly encourage them to part with their millions.

As he glanced at his reflection in the floor-length window it struck him how far he had come from the days when just finding money to support himself and his little sister had been a struggle. Resplendent in an immaculately tailored Dolce & Gabbana tuxedo cut from the finest Italian wool, he looked like he belonged.

Oliver rubbed his hand over his pecs, powerfully aware of the Maori-inspired tattoo coiled over his shoulder that the crisp white linen of his shirt concealed. His hands pulsed with renewed conviction. It was his touchstone—a symbolic reminder that he was fierce and untouchable—a warrior businessman and an impenetrable lover.

On a good day, he even fooled himself.

But no matter how easy it was to make millions, no matter how many things he acquired, he'd never found a sense of contentment.

Except with—

Oliver bit down on his teeth, grinding them together in a futile attempt to crush memories he was determined not to revisit.

He glanced at his Rolex. 7:03:02. Irritability coursed through his veins. What the hell was the auctioneer waiting for? He fixed him with a piercing look, firing his unspoken annoyance through the crowd.

Tardiness was something he abhorred, and doubly-so tonight, he thought as he locked on the important call he had to make. In one hour it would be 8am in New Zealand and his sister, as punctual as he was, would be anxiously waiting.

As though feeling the pointed tip of Oliver's anger the auctioneer looked up. His relaxed smile quickly shattered as he was forced to confront the aggressive glint in Oliver's eyes, the rigid set of his shoulders, the brutally hard line of his jaw.

The auctioneer banged his hardwood gavel on the sounding block with short urgent thuds, his florid face ballooning as the chatter continued.

"Ladies and gentlemen, can I have your attention?" More insistent hammering. "Attention! Attention!"

The chatter fell to an orderly whisper, extinguished finally by the auctioneer's solemn voice.

"As you know, tonight is a unique opportunity to savour the extraordinary passions of Oliver Hart. Renowned as an astute businessman, Oliver Hart is also an obsessive collector," he said.

"He has one of the most significant collations of contemporary art in the world. Not only a man of significant wealth, Oliver Hart, founder of Hart Luxury Hotel Consortium, is a man of outstanding generosity. All the funds raised by tonight's art auction will provide relief for those affected by last month's devastating earthquake in New Zealand, where he spent much of his childhood."

Oliver studied his feet as a thunder of applause quaked through the room, amplifying as it echoed off the walls.

Childhood.

The word was like a vicious punch to his stomach. Oppressive memories pounded his brain, and this time there was no silencing them.

Suddenly he was four years old again. Four years old and frightened. Lonely. Abandoned. Trapped in a jungle of strangers. Abandoned by bickering parents into a boarding school, neither one willing to let the other have custody. Selfishly caring more about winning against each other than the needs of their own child. And then there was his father.

His jaw locked as he bit down hard, swallowing a toxic cocktail of grief and anger. The brutal beatings hadn't hurt nearly as much as the verbal abuse and discouragement he'd suffered when he told them he wanted to be like his grandfather and study butterflies. The abuse had only intensified when he turned his back on the legal career his father had wanted. '*You'll never achieve anything. I wish you'd never been born. How dare you defy me you worthless piece of shit,*' the pain of these beatings had long healed—but those words still hurt.

Freezing sweat clung to Oliver's body in a vice-like grip, as he recalled the scorn his father rained upon him during his few personal visits. He paced across to the open window, inhaling deeply as he struggled to rip himself free from the shards of the past. Jesus, what sort of father tries to have his son institutionalised?

To some, it might seem ironic that he should be so generous to a country where he spent such an unhappy childhood, but Oliver didn't like to think of others suffering.

He forced his mind back to the present.

"Tonight's opening painting *Butterfly Lovers* is a significant artwork," the auctioneer continued, glancing down at his notes.

Oliver didn't have to read his words to know that what he would reveal was a shallow rendition of the truth. Only two people in the world truly knew just what *Butterfly Lovers* meant.

He glanced around the room thinking Ruby might have come, hoping with all his willpower she hadn't.

CHAPTER TWO

HE FORCED HIMSELF NOT TO BETRAY THE turmoil of emotions jack-knifing through his body as the massive painting was carried to the makeshift podium.

The butterfly theme had held so much promise. He'd never really bought into Ruby's tales about the transformative power of art to heal. But back then privately he'd hoped her optimism might rub off. With her by his side, and by owning the painting, perhaps he could shed a skin, free himself of his deformed past, re-emerge in a new skin. Undamaged. Someone nearing perfection. A better man. The sort of man Ruby deserved.

He'd been a fool.

Oliver's spine stiffened. He'd intended to keep it . . .

her . . . forever. But even good intentions couldn't make up for a lifetime's inability to commit. He moved towards the terrace, widening the distance between him and the painting. He would no longer succumb to the painting's potent power to remind him of his failings.

"Created specifically for Oliver over seven years ago by struggling contemporary artist CG Tombly—only Oliver could have foreseen its financial potential."

Oliver's brow furrowed. The suggestion he had acquired the painting for commercial gain, rankled him. If he wasn't such a private man he might have told the crowd the truth. He'd made the mistake of talking candidly once before—a mistake he wouldn't be making again.

In its place, he'd created a new habit—a habit of keeping his emotional life to himself, one he wasn't about to break. Soon the painting, and the painful memories of the only woman capable of making him feel, would be shed and he could devote himself to less painful obsessions.

"As always, Oliver's timing is impeccable. The painting's value has rocketed in the same soaring capacity as the palatial hotel Oliver's company has recently constructed in Dubai–so high it almost touches the gods."

The auctioneer flung his hands into the air to accentuate his point. "Oliver Hart," he said, nodding in his direction and pointing to his towering 6-foot, 2-inch frame, "never does anything small."

Oliver thrust his hands in his pockets and glanced out the window refusing to look at the painting as the bidding began.

In a few fist-clenching minutes it would all be over and he could get on with his life.

His gaze drifted to the sculpture garden, lying beyond the pool, alighting on a solitary bronze sculpture by Brancusi. The modernist interpretation of Hercules holding the world on his shoulders, with its roughly hewn egg-shaped sphere symbolising earth had always appealed to him.

Balanced precariously on a towering sculpted wood base, the odd shape and the large crater severing the middle of the sphere challenged conventional notions of perfection and reminded him of humanity's rawness.

As his gaze lingered over the sculpture it occurred to him that repairing his scars, so deep that no relationship he started ever endured, required a Herculean effort.

No wonder the painting had failed.

But he still wanted to believe, as the ancient Greeks had, that art had a powerful ability to transform lives. He only hoped that selling the painting finally fulfilled this purpose. Perhaps then the painful memories that still haunted him could be turned to good.

He turned and fixed his gaze upon the audience. Who would be its new owner he wondered as the opening bid of one million was made. Would it go to Don Hermes, the impotent pharmaceutical giant, standing just ahead of him, or some other equally innocuous purchaser? Or would some anonymous bidder calling from China, Europe or the Middle East be the lucky buyer?

"$12 million? Do I have $12 million?" The bags under the auctioneer's eyes shifted as he tilted his head forward, and peered under his glasses.

"A small price to pay," he continued, his gaze briefly flickering to Oliver, "for a painting personally commissioned by a man who defies every category and transcends every cliché: a man with tremendous gusto and creative generosity."

The auctioneer's eyes flew to a scantily dressed blonde hovering hopefully next to Oliver. "A man who has yet to be pinned down."

Oliver caste her a dismissive look and moved further toward the back of the room.

"$12 million we have," cried the auctioneer's assistant, nodding vigorously as he pressed his iPhone firmly to his ear.

Oliver's heart lurched as the bidding began.

"$13 million," the assistant taking telephone bids shouted, raising his hand.

"$13.2 million." The auctioneer's eyes darted between the phone bidder and two men determined to claim the painting as their own.

Explosive tension hovered as one of the two remaining bidders turned their attention away.

"$13.5 million! At $13.5 million the painting will be sold," the auctioneer warned. He suspended the gavel in the air, pausing as he scanned the room.

"$17.4 million," came a guttural, low growl from the front of the crowd.

A record price!

The room fell silent under the weight of the bid, then buzzed with irritatingly discordant voices, their murmurs of awe and envy a rising tide of white noise.

Oliver's eyes darted to the front row. Over $14 million? The price was ridiculous. Someone must want it desperately. But who and why?

He was acquainted with the deep pockets of unbridled obsession. He understood intimately the seductive power of the painting.

But this was crazy bidding.

There had to be a compelling reason surpassing the usual appreciation of any art-lover. At that price it could hardly be an investment buy.

So that left . . . what?

Oliver paced the back of the room in agitation unable to see the face of the man who had placed this latest bid. He caught a glimpse of the woman next to the anonymous bidder as she shook a sexy spill of sun-kissed curls down her back. The familiar gesture sent shockwaves to his heart.

It couldn't be.

Her head turned slightly.

Oliver stood still, as if turned to stone.

Ruby Diaz.

His Ruby.

CHAPTER THREE

A SYMPHONY OF EMOTIONS CRASHED through his veins as he saw a possessive arm snake around Ruby's waist and realized with horror the identity of the serpent she was with. Oliver threw back his shoulders, his muscular jaw tilted forward in defiance as he looked at the nauseatingly familiar figure.

Carlos Torres, the New York based, Mexican banking magnate and the-soon-to-be owner of *Butterfly Lovers.*

He could not let his painting—their painting—fall into her lover's clutches—a man as unscrupulous as he was deceptively charming.

Oliver's overactive mind raced with scenarios. He could draw from his own accounts the money for the earthquake fund—adding to the millions he had already donated.

But he knew with chilling certainty he was powerless to flout protocol, to bend the rules, to manipulate the outcome to suit his own desires. He knew only too well that once the auction had started, *Butterfly Lovers* could not be withdrawn.

"At this price, we'll sell," the auctioneer's eyes swept the room for any last bids.

The muscles in Oliver's chest tightened as he saw the auctioneer's gavel ascend into the air.

He watched helplessly as Carlos pulled Ruby toward him and folded her into his arms. The bitter taste of jealousy flooded his mouth.

The gavel sank toward the sounding block with freeze-frame inevitability. A splintering crack as wood met wood confirmed it was over with chilling clarity.

Oliver's hand tightened into a closed fist, crumpling the *Butterfly Lovers* catalog into obscurity.

His heart rate pulsated making his chest feel as though it was about to implode, as Ruby turned and he watched with shock the way she wilted under Carlos's dominant presence, the light of passion missing from her eyes. She seemed sad and vulnerable—and the Ruby he knew was neither.

Something was wrong.

His rational mind thundered a warning. Don't get involved.

What business was it of his if she wanted to make a life with that snake? None. Not ordinarily. But Ruby wasn't ordinary. Accepting and accommodating maybe, but something told him there was more to their union than met the eye.

He clenched his fists and cursed softly fighting against the impulse to save her from a big mistake. Playing rescuer would invite complications he didn't need.

Especially now.

What he needed was a distraction. What he needed was uncomplicated sex—not to reignite an obsession. Ruby had already proven herself capable of breaking his heart mercilessly.

Not so with paintings and sculptures and his beloved butterflies, he mused, forcing his thoughts back to his collections. Once possessed they would never leave without his consent. And he could never make them cry. His jaw clenched as bitter memories of his parents' feuding pounded in his ears. His mother's heart-wrenching cries once heard, never forgotten.

He must not be distracted. He must not allow Ruby to get close. Obviously she had engineered Carlos to buy the painting, knowing full well how it would torture Oliver. She tortured him all those years ago and it was clear she intended to continue the onslaught. She could have that damned painting, he mused as unwelcome, undesired, uncontrollable passions, long forgotten but now unbridled, threatened to escape.

He rested one shoulder against the panoramic window, his attention locked on Ruby as she freed herself from Carlos's clutches and fluttered through the swelling crowd toward the patio.

She possessed an innate and natural elegance that caused his glands to salivate, wetting his appetite in open defiance of his will. Her legs screamed danger—their long, slender length accented in scorchingly sharp stilettos that threatened to kill.

Kill his resolve. Kill his self-control. Kill him all over again.

He reached for a glass of whiskey from a passing waitress. He rocked the glass from side to side and studied the rough ice-chunks crashing through the amber liquid, then knocked the drink back, drowning his conflicting emotions.

Like a moth drawn to light he savoured the way her floor-length, silk dress clung to her lithe figure, her hibiscus red dress shimmering under the halogen lights like the wings of a newly emerged butterfly.

The way the vibrant colour of her dress contrasted so deliciously with the flock of black cocktail dresses and designer dark suits everyone else favoured brought a smile to his lips. Ruby had always stood out from the crowd.

Walk away, stay away. The voice in his head pitched high and shrill like an ambulance siren, as he fought an instinctive need to free her from a bad mistake.

The irregularly cut crystal pressed into his fingers as he gripped the glass. His life had rapidly become complicated.

He craned his neck as he momentarily lost sight of her, searching over the sea of heads and glittering diamonds.

Like the shards of ice in his glass, his hardened intention to stay detached was fracturing.

Plastering on a face of extreme nonchalance, he pushed determinedly towards her through the crowd as she stepped onto the patio and gazed forlornly up at the stars.

Why the hell was she with a dickhead like Carlos.

Glancing at his watch, Oliver wondered if he could find out what he needed to know in less than 20 minutes?

DID YOU ENJOY READING THIS EXCERPT?. . .

Thank you for purchasing and reading my books. You are more than my livelihood—you let me live my passion. Without your love of romance and belief in the power of love, this book would never have been born. I really hope you loved this excerpt from my full-length novel *Flight of Passion* as much as I enjoyed writing it.

Purchase the full-length copy and discover what happens next.

DID YOU ENJOY READING THIS EXCERPT?. . .

FLIGHT OF PASSION: BOOK ONE IN THE TRUE LOVE SERIES AVAILABLE IN PRINT, EBOOK AND AUDIO NOW FROM ALL GOOD BOOKSTORES

EXCERPT: STOLEN BY THE SHEIKH

PART I
PREQUEL: STOLEN BY THE SHEIKH

STOLEN BY THE SHEIKH

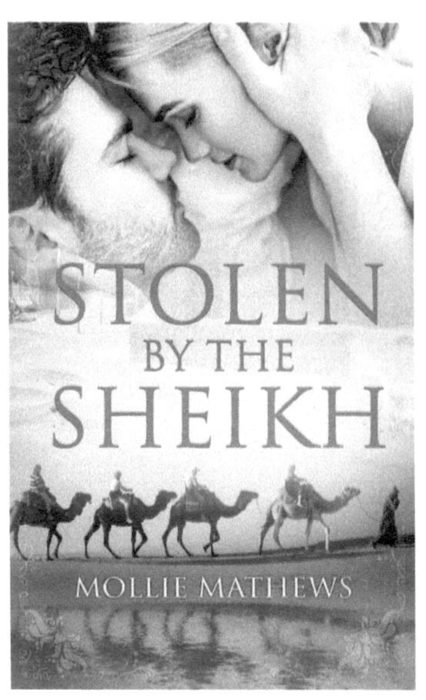

CHAPTER ONE

"Did you paint that? It's incredible. I'm in awe." The man's deep velvet voice held just a trace of a Middle-Eastern accent and the tone made Lucy blush. Not because of the compliment, but the way the man's voice resonated with every artery in her heart. If there was a sexier voice in the world she'd never heard it.

Barely conscious of the crowd pressing around her Lucy's heart quickened as she scanned the tall, dark, thoroughly captivating stranger, trailing her eyes the length of his 6 foot two inch frame. Broad-shouldered and formidable, the starkly moulded framework of his face spotlighted by the curated gallery lights. He exuded authority and a compelling magnetism that sent her pulse soaring.

Clutching the exhibition catalogue to her chest Lucy turned from him and swept her gaze over the crowd crammed into the art gallery. Pulse pounding, she tried to catch the attention of Issy Riley, the art therapist, who had encouraged her to paint her way to healing. But Issy was deep in conversation with her husband, Massimilliano Balforni, CEO of

Emporio Balforni, Milan's most prestigious fashion house, the man Issy had met and married after helping him heal his wounds too.

Lucy loved the easy way they were together and the deep love they obviously shared. She wished she could have a love like that. A love that weathered even the roughest storm. A love that shone with such a bright light.

Heat shot through her as her awareness returned to the absurdly handsome stranger beside her. Lucy shifted her gaze from Issy and Max and fixed her sight on the stark white wall closest to the door. On the white panel was her name in gold letters, Lucy Ford, and the title of the show, *The Lightkeeper's Lover*.

"Of course you painted it," the stranger said, following her gaze momentarily, before turning to her, his dark umber eyes magnetically pulling hers to his. "This is a solo exhibition and you are the star."

They both smiled, as though sharing in the surprise of their chance encounter and immediate attraction, causing her heart to somersault.

"The weather blew me in," he said, as though offering an explanation.

She looked over the sea of heads to the sky, watching in fascination as the violet-grey clouds swirled angrily outside. Gaining momentum. Faster. And faster.

Just as they had—

Lucy's breath caught in her chest as her thoughts travelled back to that haunting night so many years ago. Back to that desolate evening when she had wandered the clifftops, straddled between wanting to live and wanting to die. Back to that night when she had been rescued from the fate that was never meant to be hers.

Why had this bastion of strength come striding into her life? It was if the heavens had sought to intervene again—orchestrating the elements to throw them together.

CHAPTER TWO

"The title of your show drew me, and I was curious. Then I saw your paintings—wow! What can I say. It's exactly how it is. You've captured the emotion exactly."

"You're being kind," Lucy said, unused to such direct praise. Unexpectedly, her eyes pooled with tears. She didn't know why. She just hoped she wouldn't cry.

"No, really. The desolation. The loneliness. The isolation. But also the connection. You've taken it further, you've seen below the surface—the hope, the healing, and the beauty."

His gaze from her to the painting at the entrance, running along the soaring cliffs troughed on the canvas with a hurtle of white and ochre and veins of gold. His gaze honed in on the hauntingly beautiful face of a woman, infused within the rocks. Then rose along the formidable shaft of the lighthouse, its beam of light towering over her like a protector.

"You have a rare ability to capture emotion," he said, turning to her again. "I knew you had to be mine." Dark eyes, deep and solid as crystal held her spellbound.

He laughed, the sort of easy laugh that only those with

supreme confidence in themselves managed when revealing their unconscious thoughts. "What I meant was, I knew I had to buy one of your paintings and make it mine."

He gestured toward the largest painting on display by the door, shining like a beacon, attracting people struggling along the streets away from the wild Wellington winds and raging rain battering them mercilessly.

At just over two meters high, the painting was exactly the same commanding height as her admirer.

Lucy felt a tug of conflict, a type of regret but also pleasure as the gallery owner placed a red sticker below the painting. She had priced it ridiculously high to deter purchasers. It was special to her and she had wanted to keep it.

That painting, and the others in the collection, had saved her life. Creativity had brought healing. Art had healed her pain. But she was glad it was going to this quietly handsome, solid man with the commanding presence. There was something reassuringly familiar about him, something she couldn't quite place.

"Have we met before?" they both blurted.

Lucy shook her head, sending a curtain of blonde glossy hair sweeping across her backless little black dress. A smile fluttered to her lips, as in a reckless moment she wondered how soft his fingers would be, how supple they would feel, how sensuous the sound his skin upon her skin would be. Her body exploded in a heated flood of anticipation.

"I just, I don't know, there's something about you. Something familiar," he said.

His gaze locked with hers as though he'd sensed her silent desire. Rather than look away she felt hypnotically drawn to his light.

"Yes, it's strange. I know, but I don't know," she said.

There's something deliciously, reassuringly familiar, she thought.

"Déjà vu," he said.

"What do you mean?"

"The feeling that one has lived the present situation before."

She felt suddenly adrift, like a ship in tumultuous seas.

"You're very knowledgeable about lighthouses," Lucy said, steering the conversation to solid ground, still intrigued by the depth of his earlier conviction.

"I should be. I was the lightkeeper at Pencarrow for three years," he hesitated and gazed at the painting.

Instinct told her something deeply personal had happened to him, something that could shed light on his own traumatic past.

"After my wife died," he offered by way of explanation, "My heart was ripped apart, and the only thing that saved me was running that lighthouse. It healed my heart."

A glaze of silent understanding united them muting the noise and clatter of the crowd, guiding them both away from the jagged coastlines of their shared sorrow, pain and hurt, to the deep still waters flooding their hearts.

"I am Anwar," he said, holding out his hand with a gesture that shouted royalty. "Anwar na Hassir," he added, looking at her as though searching for some sign of recognition that his name meant something to her.

Should it?

Anwar na Hassir? He was clearly from Arabic descent but beyond that she could not place him. She barely had time to troll through her memories before the gallery owner rushed to her side.

"Lucy, come and meet another buyer—if I may steal her away?" He added, aware of his intrusion.

She turned to leave. Their sacred union temporarily shattered by the ill-timed request.

"I'll take them all," Anwar said suddenly, with an air of explosive command.

"The paintings?" the gallery owner asked. "All of them?"

Lucy's pulse rate ricocheted as Anwar nodded his agreement. Had the paintings incited something deep within his soul, she wondered? Was that why he was buying out the whole exhibition? Was he a collector like many others in the gallery? A numbers man who prided himself on his many conquests and the number of artworks he possessed?

Lighthouses were rich with symbolism and conceptual meanings. She knew that better than anyone. Was the stranger attracted to the potent symbol of hope, rescue, refuge, safety and guidance? Was he offering her the same salvation, security, and strength? Or by buying her creations did he think she was also for purchase?

As the gallery owner scuttled away to tally his commission, Lucy gripped the edge of her catalogue, unsure whether to follow or stay.

No, she reassured herself, listening to her intuition as she studied him. Rising tall above her petite frame, he represented the best of man, he harboured the most lofty of ideals. His very proximity made her feel ever closer to the heavens and God. A towering signpost to guide the way which led to eternal love.

Anwar reached out, and gently caught her hand. He cupped his fingers around hers. Every whisper of hair on her body rose in heightened awareness.

"Don't go."

It was all she needed to hear. It was all she needed to know. It was all that she needed to believe.

Dreams do come true. And keepers are forever.

* * *

THE END

Did you enjoy reading this prequel?
***Stolen by the Sheikh* due for release, 2020.**
Follow me on Bookbub and subscribe to my newsletter and be the first to know.

Follow me on Bookbub and subscribe to my newsletter and be the first to know.

ISBN eBook 978-0-9941412-4-8

ISBN print 978-0-9941412-5-5

Cover Design: © Steven Novak

Published by

Blue Orchid Publishing New Zealand

Blue Orchid
PUBLISHING

ABOUT THE AUTHOR

MOLLIE MATHEWS is a New Zealand author who writes fun, sophisticated, passion-filled contemporary romance. She is known for her "sensual, beautiful, empowered stories enveloped in true romance" (5-star review). Her books have resonated with a global audience. She has been featured in magazines, television, and radio.

A former child and family therapist Mollie passionately believes in the power of romance to transform people's lives. She loves Mother Theresa's words, "*We are all pens in the hands of a writing God sending love letters to the world.*"

Her stories are unashamedly positive, optimistic, full of fun and passion.

She is graduate of Victoria University, in Wellington, New Zealand and has given keynote speeches at romance writers conventions and international seminars.

Mollie follows the sun, dividing her time between New Zealand and exotic locations—wherever she intends setting her next romance novel. She lives with her very own romantic hero, Lorenzo—tall, dark, terribly handsome and fluent in Spanish!

Follow her on BookBub https://www.bookbub.com/authors/mollie-mathews and on her blog https://molliemathews.wordpress.com

and sign up for Mollie's newsletter at www.Molliemathews.com and receive her FREE gift.

Be inspired by Mollie on Instagram www.instagram.com/molliemathewsauthor

Follow Mollie on twitter at www.twitter.com/molliemathewsnz

Join Mollie on Facebook at www.facebook.com/molliemathewsnz

Check out her inspiration board on Pinterest www. nz.pinterest.com/molliemathews/

BY MOLLIE MATHEWS

GEMSTONE BILLIONAIRE BRIDES:

THE ITALIAN BILLIONAIRE'S CHRISTMAS BRIDE

THE ITALIAN BILLIONAIRE'S SCANDALOUS MARRIAGE

GEMSTONE BILLIONAIRES 2 BOOK-BUNDLE BOX SET

GEMSTONE BILLIONAIRES 3 BOOK-BUNDLE BOX SET

PASSION DOWN UNDER:

MARRIED BY CHRISTMAS
BRIDE OF GOLD

TRUE LOVE:

FLIGHT of PASSION
CLAIMED by THE SHEIKH
SEX WITH STRANGERS

PASSION DOWN UNDER SASSY SHORT STORIES:

FINDING A HUSBAND
TWIST OF FATE
LOVE ME FOREVER
LOVE ME AS I AM
FOREVER AND ALWAYS
THE LIGHTKEEPER'S LOVER
PASSION DOWN UNDER 2 BOOK-BUNDLE BOX SET (Books 1 & 2)
PASSION DOWN UNDER 3 BOOK-BUNDLE BOX SET (Books 1, 2 & 3)